Sir George Prevost

The Autobiography of Isaac Williams, B.D.

Fellow and Tutor of Trinity College, Oxford

Sir George Prevost

The Autobiography of Isaac Williams, B.D.
Fellow and Tutor of Trinity College, Oxford

ISBN/EAN: 9783337015305

Printed in Europe, USA, Canada, Australia, Japan

Cover: Foto ©Raphael Reischuk / pixelio.de

More available books at **www.hansebooks.com**

THE AUTOBIOGRAPHY

OF

ISAAC WILLIAMS, B.D.

a

THE AUTOBIOGRAPHY

OF

ISAAC WILLIAMS, B.D.

FELLOW AND TUTOR OF TRINITY COLLEGE, OXFORD

AUTHOR OF SEVERAL OF THE "TRACTS FOR THE TIMES"
"A COMMENTARV ON THE GOSPEL NARRATIVE," ETC.

EDITED BY HIS BROTHER-IN-LAW

THE VEN. SIR GEORGE PREVOST

LATE ARCHDEACON OF GLOUCESTER

AS THROWING FURTHER LIGHT ON THE HISTORY
OF THE OXFORD MOVEMENT

LONDON

LONGMANS, GREEN, & CO.

AND NEW YORK: 15 EAST 16th STREET

1892

EDITOR'S PREFACE

THE Editor has preserved the Author's original preface as showing the real purpose and essential character of the autobiography as written by the Author for his children. Very little has been suppressed, and in most cases only what was of a private nature.

Some of the Editor's own recollections of the great actors in the movement are inserted here and there in notes, and especially of John Keble. But he clings to the hope that some time or other the life and principal letters of the great saint and religious poet of the present century may be given to the Church. For he must ever earnestly long and pray that John Keble may be made known to the present and future generations, as he was known by them who, like the Author and the Editor, had the privilege of being with him, when cheerfully joining in the joys of young people, and also in graver hours when his far-seeing eye saw the dark clouds rising, and yet more when at last cruel disappointments of the hopes, that he had at one time ventured to cherish, *seemed* to have come upon him and his friends.

Still, the spirit of resignation never forsook him—

> " Though dearest hopes were faithless found,
> And dearest hearts were bursting round."

One cannot but think of what Hooker says of St. Athanasius, bk. v., ch. xlii. § 5 ; though, thank God, it was not " only in " John Keble that, throughout the course of that long and sad history, " nothing is observed other than such as very well became a wise man to do, and a righteous man to suffer."

MY DEAR CHILDREN,

If any of you should live to manhood, you will be glad to know something of the history of my life, and the more so, as parts of it have been spent among persons and circumstances in themselves of some interest and moment, and such as must have some effect on the future character and history of the Church in this country.

I am therefore about to set down for you in writing a few memorials of the past, which I may not live to communicate to you in any other way, when any of you shall be of years to understand them.

ISAAC WILLIAMS.

STINCHCOMBE,
December 10, 1851.

THE AUTOBIOGRAPHY

OF

ISAAC WILLIAMS, B.D.

I was born[1] at Cwmcynfelin,[2] where my mother was in the habit of staying occasionally with her father, but my early years were mostly spent in London, from the fact of my father being engaged as a Chancery barrister in Lincoln's Inn. We lived at a corner of Bloomsbury Square, in a small street, where, I believe, Newman also must have been living at the same time, though I knew nothing then of himself and his family. I had two brothers older than myself, and one younger, my

[1] Dec. 12, 1802.
[2] Near Aberystwith, Cardiganshire.

sister being the youngest of all. We had a tutor named Polehampton, an Eton man, and of King's College, Cambridge. After some time he engaged himself to live in the country as curate to a Fellow of Eton named Roberts, in a parish named Worplesdon, near Guildford, and proposed that we should go and live with him. This we did, together with two sons of Dr. Willis, the rector of Bloomsbury, our parish in London. Mr. Polehampton soon afterwards added to this number of pupils, till it became fifteen, at which it always continued. They were all boys intended for Eton, except ourselves. At this school we had everything that boys would wish for at that age—a garden for each of us, rabbits, donkeys, cricket, and other out-of-door games. Under that master I first derived a liking for Latin verse. I remember his once mentioning a reward he would give to the first boy who would bring him a copy of Latin verses out of his own head, and my greatly surprising him and anticipating his intentions by almost immediately producing a copy. But my recollections of that school upon the whole are such, that I never could send a child to a private school. Almost the first boys I came in contact with, on leaving home, produced on my mind a very startling impression. I remember then feeling, for the first time, that I understood what the Bible and the Catechism meant by speaking of the world as "wicked." In early childhood I was often much affected with strong impressions on the shortness of life, and the transitory nature of all human things, and was greatly taken with Sherlock on Death, sentences of which haunted me like some musical strain.

From this school I went to Harrow, where I enjoyed much freedom and happiness, more perhaps than was good for one. We boarded in the house of an aged clergyman, who only admitted about six; lived in his family with every home comfort in a house commanding that very extensive prospect from Harrow towards London. We had each of us his little study, so small as only to admit of one companion. At Harrow I should have spent my time very idly, playing much at cricket and such games, were it not that I took great delight in Latin exercises, especially Latin verse; and my ambition, too, was excited in getting prizes and boyish admiration. When in the sixth form, where we were left much at liberty to select any mode of treating a given thesis, I used to stay awake in bed, and so would do a whole exercise, committing it to paper in the morning, to the surprise of those companions who knew I had left it all undone on the evening before. And so much was I used even to think in Latin, that, when I had to write an English theme, which was very rarely, I had to translate my ideas, which ran in Latin, into English.

My great bane at Harrow was the very warm and strong attachments I formed with boys not in every case of the best principles. But my one great friend latterly was a boy who came to Harrow with very singular promise, having published a volume of poems at the age of eleven, and another at fourteen, and the Percy Anecdotes on the subject of " Youth " were at that time dedicated to him, with his picture in the frontispiece; he was introduced to the Duke of Wellington, and extremely flattered and ad-

mired, especially by his own father, Sir
G. Dallas. He was at that time one of
great tenderness of mind, but of peculiar
fastidious refinement. He is the present
Sir Robert C. Dallas. We went to Oxford
to be entered together, his father accom-
panying us, and we at first lived much
together in Oxford, although he was of
Oriel College and I of Trinity.

The great charm of my life at Harrow
was composition, especially Latin, and our
exercises were so numerous—four every
week—that I then acquired the habit of
writing so much. In our school library
there was an elegant edition of his poems
which Lord Byron had given, having been
himself educated at Harrow. Into these
poems I ventured to look, feeling at the
time that I ought not to do so, but was
most agreeably surprised by finding so
very little harm in them ; indeed, nothing

but what *I thought* one might read with safety, and from this was but a slight step to great admiration. The subtle poison of these books did me incalculable injury for many years; the more so as the infidelity was so veiled in beautiful verse and refined sentiment. To counteract all these and the like temptations at that most important period of life, I received at Harrow no religious instruction whatever of any kind, and the place in church, where the lower school sat at that time, was in a gallery of the side aisle, where it was impossible to hear any part of the service. Happy as my youth was at Harrow, and much pained as I was to leave it, yet I earnestly pray God that He will prolong my life for the education of my own children, that they may never go to any school, although I consider our great public schools better than smaller and private schools, from my own experience; and although I am aware that selfishness and ambition are more fostered by home-education, yet the atmosphere of a public school must be very different from what it then was to be suitable for a Christian child.[1]

At Harrow there were speech days, one in each of the three summer months, when the senior boys recited set speeches before a large company. On the opening of the new schools, when I was there, three prizes were appointed to be given annually from that time. I was writing for the Latin, when I was called away to attend the funeral of my grandfather in Wales. I put what I had done into the hands of a

[1] He must ultimately have modified his views as to the comparative benefits and temptations connected with home and school education, for at last he sent his children to large schools, Marlborough, Winchester, etc.—(Editor's note.)

friend, to write out and send in for me ;
and on my return from Wales found that
my poem was one of the successful three.
The next year—no one being allowed to
succeed twice for the same prize—I was
allowed to be a candidate only for the
other two prizes, the Greek and Latin
Lyrics ; and was again inopportunely sent
home, and there laid up with a fever, in
London.   But the subjects continued in
my mind, and as soon as I was able to write,
I sent them to a friend at Harrow, one
with the motto "velut ægri somnia vanæ
finguntur species." And both my poems
were successful, to the surprise of all the
school, who thought I had been removed by
my illness from the scene of competition.

Had it not been for this love of composition, I was at this time rather an idle
than a studious boy ; being one of the
chief cricketers at the school, and taken

c

up with the fascinations of the society I was falling into in the families of those boys who were my chief friends. We in the sixth form looked with great admiration on our head master, Dr. Butler; and my tutor, Henry Drury, who was then very famous for his library, was an eminent classical scholar; but the tastes of the two were so very different, that one would often praise the same exercise and select it for commendation, which the other had as strongly condemned. But both gave great encouragement to one ambitious of such excellence. I cannot recall my feelings at that period without emotion : something within me would have expanded the heart to everything great and good; but it was not so. I was surrounded with alluring temptations and flattered, with no one in that little opening world to guide me or speak of Christianity. I was entered at

Trinity College by Henry Drury, against my father's wishes, who was desirous of what he would have thought a better college for me, and on going to reside there I found a nephew of H. Drury's, a scholar of the college, was engaged by him as my private tutor, but from this unprofitable connection I disengaged myself during the year. Being thus placed at Trinity, I found in the second term of my residence that scholarships of the college were thrown open to competition and to be contested for. I stood and was elected; there were no able competitors. The habits suitable to a scholar's gown in some degree tended to break my connection with my more gay Harrow associates; my ties with Dallas were in some degree loosened. But at this exceedingly miserable period of my life, when I was as one already utterly lost, although in good estimation outwardly among men, yet with ruin within me, almost irretrievably fixed, a very merciful and wondrous Providence was bringing about, by apparently slight accidents, the turning-point of my whole life.

There was an excellent old clergyman living at Aberystwith, Mr. Richards, who had been once curate of Fairford, and he promised to introduce me to John Keble, who was then a tutor at Oriel, on the first opportunity, the Kebles having been acquainted with my father. This summer, 1822, John Keble came to see his old friend, Mr. Richards, at Aberystwith; I was introduced to him, and rode with him on his returning home the chief part of the way to the Devil's Bridge, amidst that scenery which suggested, I believe, at that time the hymn for the twentieth Sunday after Trinity.

I should here mention that Cwm Cynfelin, in Wales, had now become our home, as much as London ; my grandfather had at his death left a very large estate, to be divided between his two daughters—my mother, who was the eldest, and her sister, Mrs. General Davies. But it was for some years the subject of an expensive and harassing lawsuit respecting the division.

I saw nothing of John Keble, after returning to Oxford, and thought he had forgotten me, till a year had nearly ex- pired, when I succeeded in getting the Latin verse prize, " Ars Geologica." He then appeared in my rooms, on the ground- floor opposite the garden at Trinity, and said he had come to ask whether he could assist me in looking over my prize poem before it was printed and recited. On looking it over with him, I was exceedingly amazed at his remarks, and said, on coming away, Keble has more poetry in his little finger than Milman in his whole body. For Milman was then the great poet of Oxford, and, as Poetry Professor, he also had been looking over my poem with me. But on venturing to quote Keble's opinion at that time to my tutor at Trinity, he said, " John Keble may understand Aristotle, but he knows nothing of poetry. It is out of his line."

This occurred, of course, just before the Long Vacation, when the poems are recited at Oxford ; and, humanly speaking, I was still without any chance or prospect of a change of life. Influences of school and college had done very much to undo the blessed inspirations of childhood, home instructions, and maternal warnings ; and the eye of God set in the soul at Baptism had well-nigh withdrawn itself, although still all was fair without and of good report, which renders man more loathsome in the sight of God.   But it so happened—by the gracious ordering of Him, who disposeth all things—that I was detained in Oxford, after the vacation had commenced, in order to go up for my Little Go Examination. And when left alone in the college, Keble came to see me, and walking with him out of my rooms, I happened to mention that I had no plan for reading during the vacation, and ought to be thinking of it. After a pause he said, most unexpectedly, " I am going to leave Oxford now for good.   Suppose you come and read with me.   The Provost has asked me to take Robert Wilberforce,[1] and I declined, but, if you would come, you might be companions."   It was this very trivial accident,

---

[1] Robert Isaac Wilberforce, son of the great and good William Wilberforce, and elder brother of Samuel, Bishop, first of Oxford, and then of Winchester. —(Editor.)

this short walk of a few yards and a few words spoken, that were the turning-point of my life. If a merciful God had miraculously interposed to arrest my course, I could not have had a stronger assurance of His Presence, than I have always had in looking back to that day.

My impression is that John Keble had then been residing nine years as tutor at Oriel. He had been twice examining master, and this, with his double first-class and two prizes in the same year, invested him with a bright halo and something of awe in the eyes of an undergraduate. He was now retiring, to live on the country curacy of Southrop, a little retired village not far from Fairford, where his father and sisters resided. His mother had died just before this time, so that I never saw her.

It was a very rainy day when I travelled

outside a coach from London to Lechlade, where I slept that night, and Keble came and took me to Southrop the next morning. He said, as his house was not yet furnished, and he could not receive us, he thought of our lodging at a farmhouse, called Dean Farm, a solitary place on the Cotswold. We walked over to see it, about four miles, I think, with Froude,[1] who was also there. It was in the evening, and Keble was out when we started from Southrop. It came on a thick mist and rain, and the night was perfectly dark, and I wandered out the whole night till near the morning. The next day I was laid up, and Keble sent me a bottle of wine and other things, it being, I think,

[1] Richard Hurrell Froude, eldest son of Archdeacon Froude, and always a very dear friend of Keble, Newman, and Isaac Williams, born Lady Day, 1803, died February 28, 1836.

Sunday. For six weeks we stayed at this Dean Farm, riding over every day to Southrop, and at the end of that time Keble took us into his house, where I formed a most valued friendship with Froude. He was an Eton man, and at Oriel, of a little older standing than myself. There was an originality of thought and a reality about him which were very refreshing.

Although Oxford had made Keble so formidable, as a don and tutor usually is, yet we found ourselves with him as if he were the youngest, so that John Parker— a rude countryman who acted as clerk, gardener, and groom—used to say, "Master is the greatest boy of the lot." It was to me quite strange and wonderful that one so distinguished should always ask one's opinion, as if he was younger than myself. And one so overflowing with

real genuine love in thought, word, and
action, was quite new to me, I could
scarcely understand it. I had been used
to much gentleness and kindness, which
is so fascinating in good society, but this
was always understood to be chiefly on
the surface; but to find a person always
endeavouring to do one good, as it were,
unknown to one's self, and in secret, and
even avoiding that his kindness should
be felt and acknowledged as such, this
opened upon me quite a new world.
Religion a reality, and a man wholly
made up of love, with charms of conversation, thought, and kindness, beyond
what one had experienced among boyish
companions,—this broke in upon me all
at once. Here were many of us, taught
with much pains and care by one till then
a stranger, and altogether gratuitously,
always rejecting all idea of payment or

compensation, and this, though he could afford it less than ourselves. This was new.

At Harrow, as at other public schools, the poor were never spoken of but by some contemptuous term—looked upon as hateful boors to be fought with, or cajoled for political objects ; but for them to be looked upon with tender regard and friendship, more than the rich, and in some cases even referred to as instructors of that wisdom which God teaches them, this was a new world to me ; but, beyond all, for the wisest of the wise, and the most learned of men, to be more full of playful jest than a boy, so full of love and good nature towards all persons, of whom one might speak in conversation. Each of us was always delighted to walk with him, Wilberforce to gather instruction for the schools, and the rest of us for love's sake.

Keble had three small churches to serve--the " nine curacies," as Bishop Lloyd called them—and which he had before often served from Oxford. This long vacation at Southrop, I began Aristotle's " Ethics," which served as a foundation for instruction in religion and morals generally, more than I have ever learned from any one, on any other occasion. In addition to this I read nothing but a little of Æschylus' " Agamemnon," and was found deficient, especially in English, so much had I been used to Latin, to the neglect of English, which deficiency I feel I have never recovered. I could always have written better in Latin than in English. Keble recommended me to render the Greek into English with great care, and to learn Shakespeare by heart.

Except for a short time, when I went

to Wales and rode my horse back, I spent all this vacation at Southrop, and I think all my subsequent ones. It was, I think, on this occasion that John Keble said, "Since you have shown me your Latin poems, I shall be vain enough to show you my English ones," and he then lent me to read what has since been called "The Christian Year." It was carefully written out in small red books. I read it a great deal, but did not much enter into it. No more did Froude when he saw it ; and I think even long after he was averse to the publication of it. Among other things he said, "People will take Keble for a Methodist." At that time I told Keble my favourite poet was Collins. He said there was not enough thought in him to please himself. Froude was always maintaining some argument with Keble, occasionally some monstrous paradox. He was considered a very odd fellow at College, but clever and original; Keble alone was able to appreciate and value him. If he had not at this time fallen into such hands, his speculations might have taken a very dangerous turn; but, as his father, the archdeacon, told me, from this time it was much otherwise, he continued to throw out strong parodoxes, but always for good.

On returning to Oxford, Froude had now taken the place of my former companions, Keble being a great bond between us. I think he took more to me than I did to him, because I had been used to more of worldly refinement and sentiment; whereas he was unworldly and real. But still, we were much united, and became more and more so. In my Oxford life I now became very studious, which I had never been before, and retiring; preyed upon by secret shame and sorrow, in the new light in which I viewed myself.

It was at the next Easter, on going to Southrop, that I met, for companions there during that vacation, Hubert Cornish, Henry Ryder—the eldest son of the bishop —and Sir George Prevost. With the last I became, from the very first, great friends, and have continued to be so ever since. And thus, at Oriel, a college in which I had chiefly lived from the very first, I fell into an entirely new society, which was mostly composed of those who came from private tutors, and had not been at any public school—Anderson (now Sir C.), Boyle,[1] Robert and Samuel Wilberforce, and Henry Ryder. But Froude was not of this set.

I do not remember hearing of Pusey at this time, except that shortly after I went

[1] Father of the present Earl of Glasgow.—(Editor.)

to Oxford, I heard of him as a man who ought to have a first class made for him by himself, he being so superior to every one else in the mass of information he had acquired. Newman had been a scholar at Trinity before, but had left it, and had been elected a Fellow of Oriel before I was entered at Oxford. Once I remember to have met him when I was an undergraduate. I was invited to breakfast with William Churton, a Fellow of Oriel, and the only person I met was Newman. He did not notice me, and was talking all the while with Churton, on the subject of serving churches, and how much they would allow him for a Sunday. He had then a less refined look about him, than when I knew him afterwards. I often alluded to this occasion of meeting, but could not in any way bring it to his recollection. It is so often that the younger

E

notices and remembers his elders, while
they do not recollect him. Prevost[1] mentioned that Newman talked to him with
great admiration of Lord Byron as a poet
at their high table at Oriel, where the

---

[1] I remember this conversation very well, and it
seems due to Cardinal Newman to explain, that we
talked principally about the siege of Corinth, which
had interested me very much, and which he also
thought much superior in its moral tone to most, if
not all, of Lord Byron's other poems, though even
there he is delighting to make a hero of a bad man.
But he appeared to think that Lord Byron's great
excellence as a poet was his command of language.
He asked me to take a walk with him next day, when
we talked upon religious subjects, and I remember
that he spoke about the *gradual* revelation of great
truths in the Old Testament, especially of the resurrection of the dead. I remember also hearing him
preach about this time at the little old church of St.
Clement's, just over Magdalen Bridge. All that I
can recall of that sermon, was that he spoke in it of
the clergy as exposed to special trials and dangers
like the officers in an army, against whom the enemy
are sure especially to direct their fire. Surely this
was in some measure fulfilled in himself; at least, so
it seems to me.—(Editor's note.)

Fellows and the gentlemen Commoners dined together. This is all I remember concerning him in any way at that time.

No one has had deeper influence for good than Keble, even far beyond what is known ; for many of far other opinions, such as Dr. Arnold, yet derived from his influence what good they had. But in his intercourse then with us, almost school-boys as we were, there was such an absence of all authority or preaching of religion that it might have been asked where all this transforming power was, when there appeared nothing but affectionate play-fulness. Independent of this wonderful spell which love and humility have, I will mention one instance of things not for-gotten. Froude told me many years after that Keble once, before parting from him, seemed to have something on his mind which he wished to say, but shrunk from saying. At last, while waiting, I think, for a coach, he said to him before parting, " Froude, you said one day that Law's ' Serious Call ' was a clever " (or " pretty," I forget which) " book ; it seemed to me as if you had said the day of judgment would be a pretty sight." This speech, Froude told me, had a great effect on his after-life ; and I observed that in the published letters in " Froude's Remains," he twice alludes to it. The mention of this book reminds me of another circumstance. Robert Wilberforce, who spent one long vacation there with us, did not feel towards Keble as we did, *at that time*, having been brought up in an opposite school ; he observed one day, " What a strange person Keble is ; there is ' Law's Serious Call,' instead of leaving it about to do people good, I see he reads it and puts it out of the way, hiding it in a drawer." The same reality in religion and self-discipline, to the rejection of appearances and all pretension, had a remarkable effect on Ryder. He also had been brought up in a strict evangelical school of the better kind ; and on one occasion got up and left a college party in consequence of something that Froude had said that seemed to him to be of a light kind. But when he afterwards came to know the deep self-humiliation and depth of devotion there was in Froude's character, which was engaged in the discipline of the heart, he became so shocked with himself and his own opinions, that he adopted the opposite course. So that Keble once said of him, " Hypocrites are of two kinds: some endeavour to appear better than they are, and others worse, and Ryder is the latter." But what Ryder said was, " The idea of my setting myself up for better than others, who are so infinitely better than myself!" The fact is that Keble made humility the one great study of his life—there was such a reality and truth about him that even good men of an opposite school in religion appeared to one as counterfeits, when one was used to him ; and one felt one's self hollow from the contrast.

It was in August, 1825, that I first went with Froude into Devonshire. We went by a steamer from Cowes to Plymouth, as described in a letter in " Froude's Remains " (part I., vol. i., p. 181). From Totnes, we walked up the Dart by Dartington House to the Parsonage—that place which ever since has been to me dearer than my native vales ; of which I always say, " Ille terrarum mihi præter omnes Angulus ridet." The Froudes were eight in family, and the Archdeacon became a great friend. But the people

after my own heart were at Dartington
House. For although the Champernownes
were altogether different in natural character
from the Kebles, yet there was this same
attractive charm in them also to me at
that time, in that they were so natural and
unworldly, and therefore, in contrast to
my Harrow life, so refreshing. We often
spent the evening on the Dart, and drank
tea on the Island. Bishop Carey came at
that time to the Parsonage, with Dr. Bull.
With the Archdeacon and Hurrell we
rode along the coast, being very hospitably
entertained at different houses; and at
last from the Holdsworths' house at Dart-
mouth we came up the river Dart by boat.
My mother used to say she always liked
my being in Devonshire, as my letters
from there showed I was more happy than
anywhere else.

It was about this time that my studies

at Oxford came to a sudden and entire check. I had proceeded so well in my classics, by Keble's assistance, that I thought I was well up to what was required for a first class ; and from a foolish ambition, and against Keble's advice, I undertook to read for a first class in mathematics also. They had always been my great aversion, but by resolutely undertaking them, I soon got to like mathematics very much, and had made some progress. I was reading at that time very hard, and rising at four o'clock, I think, every morning. But, being unwell, I went to London to consult Abernethey, who told me on no account to look into any book whatever. This was to me very unfortunate and ill advice ; for, such intense study and so great a weight of reading on my mind being thus suddenly stopped, my mind turned to prey upon itself, and I became, in consequence, very ill for many years. But it was perhaps so providentially ordered that a soul, made conscious of sin through the means of a divinely-sent guide and instructor, should not be allowed to hide itself in the eager pursuits of literary objects, but be thrown upon itself, unnerved and checked for some years. A poem on the subject of this illness, written at Cwm[1] in 1826, was, in some sense, the first poem I had written in English; what little I had done before were attempts to translate into English what I had written in Latin on leaving Harrow. About this period I spent my time with Prevost at Belmont, and with Keble, who then for a short time had the curacy of Hursley[2] (I think at this time I saw the poet Southey, in Hursley Church), and was sometimes

[1] Cwmcynfelin, Cardiganshire.
[2] Of which he was afterwards for many years vicar.

F

at Dartington Parsonage. Prevost, this summer of 1826, came to Cwm and was engaged to my sister; and afterwards Froude came there too, and gives an account of his stay there in his published journal,[1] where I am mentioned under the letter I, and Prevost under that of P. All this time I was very unwell and preying on my own mind. I went to Oxford to reside my bachelor's term, and lived with Sir Charles Anderson, and saw much of Froude, who was very kind to me. I went to Dartington with the Archdeacon[2] from Oxford, and spent the Easter there. After this, I continued unwell in Wales, till Prevost and my sister were married; and, on their taking the curacy of Bisley, they came as far as Hereford to meet me, and after staying at Glo'ster for Prevost's

[1] "Froude's Remains," part I., vol. i., pp. 13-24.
[2] Archdeacon Froude, Rector of Dartington.

ordination, we went to Chalford, in Bisley parish, and became acquainted with Mr. and Mrs. Thomas Keble. After staying there three months, my sister was ordered to Hyères, in the south of France, for the winter, and I continued in Bisley parish during their absence, to look after the poor, although not yet ordained. My mother went with them. It was about this time that the sonnets, called "The Golden Valley" in the "Thoughts in Past Years," were written—and so named from the valley of that name near Chalford.

In September, 1829, I went with Thomas Keble to see the curacy of Windrush, the curacy on which he had himself been ordained fourteen years before. I was ordained on this at the following Christmas, and lived there for two years with James Davies, my vicar, who has been my most esteemed friend ever since. I was here

thrown upon myself, nothing to excite my
vanity or love of society—and the sermons
I wrote during that time are most simple,
but better I think in ἦθος than any since.
This is the place spoken of as the River's
Bank in the "Thoughts in Past Years."
At this time—about the year 1829—I
became first acquainted with the Parisian
Breviary, with which I was very much
struck, as was also John Keble, to whom
I showed the book at Fairford, which was
but a ride from Windrush. I was so
taken with the hymns, that I translated
several at that time, with no idea of
publication. The poems[1] I wrote at

---

[1] *December* 6, 1859. It is curious how things were
providentially tending in various directions towards
Catholic principles. Prevost had brought back from
Paris the four volumes of the Parisian Breviary,
which I had at Windrush, and which took me, and
John Keble too, so much by surprise. About the
same time, Palmer's "Origines Liturgicæ" were
being published, and Palmer himself came to reside

Windrush were much more simple and unpretending than what I had written in Bisley parish the year before. This was partly from the humiliation I then felt, but chiefly from the influence of the simplicity of Thomas Keble and the effect his simple sermons had on my mind ; so that

in Oxford; and Bishop Lloyd, then the Divinity Professor, was giving lectures on the Prayer-book, and referring men to the sources from whence the Prayer-book was taken, and in particular to the breviaries, on account of which copies of them were procured from a Roman Catholic bookseller in London. I have Froude's Prayer-book, a large edition interleaved, which he used for that purpose at that time. By-the-bye, when I was translating those breviary hymns for my personal edification at Windrush, there prevailed a general horror among Church people of unauthorized hymns being sung in church, and I remember I put them often into unrhythmical harsh metres to prevent this. At the same time, J. Keble was translating his Psalms, which he was very anxious should not be introduced into any church service till he had got the Archbishop's or Bishop's sanction, as the authority of the Church. —(Author's note.)

Newman afterwards, when I was his curate, said it would be better if I was more myself in my sermons, and less like Thomas Keble. Mrs. Greenaway, my parishioner at Little Barrington, also told me the same; for I had sometimes written a sermon myself, but preached one of T. Keble's instead, from distrust of myself, and thinking so much more highly of him. But this was a mistake; every body succeeds best as himself.

When I was at Windrush, there occurred some agrarian riots, and every one was much alarmed and panic struck; John Keble rode with the mob, fearlessly and good-naturedly, entreating them not to demolish the farmer's machines; they put forth a methodist preacher to answer him, as he stood on a machine begging them to desist. He wrote a little tract on the subject, in the shape of a dialogue, to express what might have been said by himself and the preacher.

About this time, or a little later, he rode over one day to Windrush, with Froude and Robert Wilberforce, to speak about a case of conscience. Lord Brougham had offered R. W. a living which Froude thought he ought not to accept. Keble and I thought there was no principle sacrificed in his doing so, as he had been used to speak highly of Brougham, and did not differ from him in principle, as we did. Froude told us that R. W. now talked very much like a High Churchman, but he did not know that he meant much by it. This I mention, as R. W. appears, since that time, so very much improved; good principles were sinking into him more and more deeply.[1] Before the end

[1] This was written several years before R. J. Wilberforce's defection to Rome, which was followed not long after by his death.—(Editor.)

of two years passed at Windrush I was elected Fellow of Trinity, and was given to understand that I must reside in the following October, and succeed to a tutorship there at once. On this I gave up my curacy, and in the interval of those few months was attacked for the first time with the asthma, which has never since left me.

My life at Windrush was very calm and subduing. I studied Hebrew, which I have not since resumed, and Chrysostom, both as devotional reading; and though living in the house with my vicar, and having our meals together, yet he was not then a companion, for our rule was always to walk in opposite directions in the parishes under our charge; and, having three churches to serve between us, we were never in church together. I lived low, my life was monotonous and very

good for me; but the relief was great
when I could get over to see the Prevosts
at Chalford, and John Keble at Fairford,
which was not very distant—I think about
twelve miles.

" The Christian Year" had then been
published for some years. I remember,
when it was first in the press, coming with
Keble out of Baxter's printing-office, when
Keble said, " It will be still-born, I know
very well; but it is only in obedience to
my father's wishes that I publish it, and
that is some comfort." I was then in
Oxford, and when it came out, and Keble
sent it to me, I was going with Prevost
(it was before his marriage) to stay at
Llandrindod Wells, where there was a
large boarding-house, and the people all
lived together. And, being in great want
of books in wet weather, after they had
been reading Lord Byron together, a

G

large party named Whitaker and their
friends requested to see my book—" The
Christian Year "—which was then perfectly fresh in my hands from the printer
and the author, and to my surprise they
were greatly delighted with it, especially
Miss Whitaker, the sister of a Harrow
friend. I mention this as the first indication of the popularity of " The Christian
Year," which I do not think I myself at
that time anticipated; certainly Froude
did not.[1] On that occasion of staying
at Llandrindod the vicar of our parish
was there—Mr. Hughes, of Aberystwith,
a Puritanical Welsh preacher. He had,
for a short time, the curacy of Dedington,
near Oxford; and speaking to me of
Oxford, he looked grave and displeased

[1] Nor did the editor. He remembers buying ten
copies of the second edition to encourage the sale
of it.—(Editor's note.)

at the mention of Keble of Oriel as being
my friend, and said it would be a great
thing for me to know a most promising
and excellent person there, Mr. Newman.
They had both, Newman and Mr. Hughes,
belonged to the Church Missionary Society,
and it was plain that he, at that time,
considered Newman to be of his own
Calvinistic party. I was myself unac-
quainted with Newman at the time of my
leaving Windrush for Oxford; but I have
a letter from Thomas Keble, of Bisley,
about that time, in which he expresses
his concern at Froude's talking of taking
Newman to Fairford to see his father, on
account of his liberal principles. This is
a curious contrast to a letter I received
from Thomas Keble about a year afterwards, strongly recommending me to
avail myself of Newman's offer for me
to be his curate, in order that I might

have more of the society of such a man.[1]

[1] *December* 8, 1859.—As a curious indication of the history of the changes in Newman's mind I was much struck in taking up these notes, with about a year's interval between—the former written to me as curate of Windrush, expressing dislike of Newman; the second written to me as Fellow of Trinity, so highly in admiration of him. But, on my mentioning the circumstance not long since to John Keble, he referred to his sister saying, "You see what Tom really meant—he wished you to be with Newman in order to keep him straight."

Perhaps there is no more extraordinary instance of the changes which Newman has undergone than in the "Home Thoughts Abroad," which Newman published in the *British Magazine* on his first going to Rome with Froude in 1831–32, for in those papers he expresses his astonishment at the exact and wonderful fulfilment of the prophecies that represented Rome and its bishop as the Antichrist, which although he had always held, he said he never could have realized, had he not witnessed its idolatries. But the next time he visited Rome it was as a Roman Catholic. Archdeacon Wilberforce mentioned to me here, before he himself joined the Church of Rome, that when Fellows of Oriel together, Pusey, Froude, himself, and Newman used to meet together on Sunday evenings when Newman

When I now went to reside in Oxford, in October, as college tutor, I felt what a great change had come on my mind since residing there before, on account of the influence of Bisley and Windrush ; and I found this the more on returning to the society of Froude, for I was become so much more soft and practical, and he more theoretical and speculative. The intellectual Oriel School, which had come through Whately, and in some degree infected Newman, was in the strongest contrast to that by which I had of late been trained. If my moral sense had been improved, not so the intellectual. And I find my Oxford sermons, for some time, were almost as simple as those at Windrush, but especially directed against the pride of intellect and the dan-

used eloquently to expound the Apocalypse, taking Mede's view, that the Pope is Antichrist.—(Author's note.)

gers of theory and mere knowledge in religion, which is altogether a matter of practice. Yet this change that had been going on, from difference of circumstances, in no way lessened my friendship and intimacy with Froude, but rather increased it; for, though naturally inclined to speculation, he was himself entirely of the Keble school, which in opposition to the Oriel or Whatelian, set $\mathring{\eta}\theta o\varsigma$ above intellect; for I always looked upon the combination of these two schools in Newman, who was first a disciple of Whately's and then of Keble's, as the cause of such disastrous effects, which have now, in him, united German rationalism with the Church of Rome, in their full developments. Living at that time so much with Froude, I was now in consequence, for the first time, brought into intercourse with Newman; we almost daily walked and dined together. Newman and Froude were, just then, turned out of their tutorships at Oriel (together with Robert Wilberforce, who left Oxford for his living of East Farleigh). Their course had, as yet, been chiefly academical; but, now released from college affairs, their thoughts were more open to the state of the Church. Our principles then were of the Caroline Divines, thinking much of the Divine right of kings, and the like; but we approached perhaps more to those of the non-jurors. Newman was now becoming a Churchman; the first thing he did publicly, which marked this change of sentiment, had been a pamphlet on the Church Missionary Society, recommending the clergy to join it, in order that, by their numbers, they might correct that Calvinistic leaven, on account of which they were opposed to it. For this pamphlet (written in apparent

simplicity as to its effect, like No. 90 afterwards), recommending that which really
would have entirely overturned that society,
he was put out of their committee, but
still continued to belong to the society.
I was greatly charmed and delighted with
Newman, who was extremely kind to me,
but did not altogether trust his opinions,
and although Froude was in the habit of
stating things in an extreme and para-
doxical manner, yet one always felt conscious of a thorough foundation of truth
and principle in him—a ground of entire
confidence and agreement—but this was
not so with Newman, even although one
appeared more in unison with his more
moderate statements. Our principles were
so little those of Newman, up to this time,
that he had been the cause of Hawkins
being elected Provost of Oriel, instead of
Keble. Newman, indeed, has sometimes

explained this to me by saying that he had looked on J. Keble like something one would put under a glass, and put on one's chimney-piece to admire, but as too unworldly for business and the things of this life. This was because he did not know him.[1] But certainly their principles were then quite opposite. But at this time he was coming to look to Keble altogether as he received him second-hand through Froude. Newman had a peculiar power of seizing intellectually the $\tilde{\eta}\theta os$ and principles of another, and making them his own, as it were on trial. I was struck with this afterwards in a remarkable manner by the way in which he learned through me the $\gamma\nu\tilde{\omega}\mu\alpha\iota$, as he called them,

[1] John Keble always laboured to keep clear of secular affairs, but when forced by duty to engage in them, he was a very good man of business. I have heard Isaac Williams say so, and all I remember confirms this statement of his.—(Editor's note.)

H

of Thomas Keble of Bisley, his character and principles; so that, at one time, when I walked daily with him, and we conversed on these subjects, I found the same views drawn out and expressed in his own way in his sermon at St. Mary's on the following Sunday. The first volume which he published is almost entirely made up of these, and will be found to differ on this account from his succeeding volumes as more practical. It has this marked distinguishable character, owing to this circumstance, and I always looked upon that volume as Bisley, passing through me, and appearing developed by Newman in St. Mary's pulpit. It was in this manner that Newman was now imbibing John Keble, through Froude, when I came to reside in Oxford. Keble's name with us always cut short every argument, so instinctively did we look to his authority.

But I always thought Froude an unfair
exponent of Keble's opinions—they were
stated by him in a manner so much his
own, so startling and original, and put in
so extreme a light, that I could hardly
recognize them as the same—so different
was his from Keble's manner of expressing
himself.[1]

Things at Oxford at that time were

---

[1] Froude used to defend his startling way of putting
facts and arguments on the ground that it was the
only way to rouse people and get their attention, and
he said that when you had once done this you might
modify your statements.   There is, of course, some
truth in this, but it always seemed, and still seems, to
me a dangerous line.   John Keble *could* not do so;
his great humility and diffidence would prevent it,
and that strict conscientiousness which hindered him
from even willingly overstating any fact, or pressing
any argument beyond what he saw it really did prove.
In that respect, as in other things also, he was a
follower of Bishop Butler.   I remember well hearing
him say that Bishop Wilson's books were the best for
people in general, and Bishop Butler's for stronger
and more cultivated intellects.—(Editor's note.)

very dead. I made it a point conscien-
tiously to attend every University sermon,
but it was a great trial of patience, and on
Saints' days I was often nearly the only
one in church listening to the usual hack
preacher, who was reading some old
sermon, not necessarily in connection with
the Saint's day, earning his five guineas
in a manner unedifying and unprofitable
to all but himself. As a proof of this I
remember this preacher—Mr. Hughes,
vicar of St. Clement's, a former scholar
of Trinity—said to Short, in our common
room, " I wonder what Williams admires
so much in me ; he is the only person in
the University who comes to my sermons
on Saints' days. It is very complimentary
of him, but it puts me to a little trouble,
for I am obliged to look out for sermons
on the day." Thus was I at that time
the only solitary silent witness for the

observance of these holy days, *i.e.* about the year 1832. Afterwards we got these Saints' days sermons, which were in the gift of the bursars of colleges, very often given to us, and obtained the appointments for the most eminent men, often Newman, sometimes J. Keble, so that when I left Oxford the University Church was filled to overflowing on Saints' days.

Froude and I seemed entirely alone, with Newman only secretly, as it were, beginning to sympathize. I became at once very much attached to Newman, won by his kindness and delighted by his good and wonderful qualities, and he proposed that I should be his curate at St. Mary's. For this my college duties would have allowed me no time; but it was agreed that I should not do very much. And this brought me into still closer intercourse with him. I have lately heard it stated from one of Newman's oldest friends, Dr. Jelf, that his mind was always essentially Jesuitical. In endeavouring to account for this statement, I can remember a strong feeling of difference I first felt on acting together with Newman, from what I had been accustomed to ; that he was in the habit of looking for effect, for what was sensibly effective, which, from the Bisley and Fairford school, I had been long habituated to avoid. I had been taught there to do one's duty in faith, and leave the effect to God, and that all the more earnestly because there were no sympathies from without to answer. There was a felt, but unexpressed, dissonance of this kind ; but perhaps it became afterwards harmonized as we acted together. What was at that time most congenial to myself were the poor at Littlemore ; it was a detached country village, belonging to St. Mary's church, but two miles from Oxford, and with no church of its own at that time. Newman had then, every Thursday evening, a lecture there in a hired room. He on these occasions expounded some passage of Scripture. Although his ideas were usually beyond the poor, yet they were always fond of his preaching, and no doubt gained much; but on taking this lecture from him I substituted, in my turn, the Church prayers and the reading of a sermon of Thomas Keble's.

Soon after I became Newman's curate the cholera came. It reached Oxford the last week in term, before the Long Vacation. It was agreed that I should take the first half of the vacation, while Newman went away. It was an awful time, from the uncertainty which then overhung the nature of the disease. Froude continued great part of the time with me in Oxford;

and my father came to stay with me. Yet still in college I was alone, and when a Fellow staying up at the adjoining college, New of St. John's, died, it appeared near. We had no case at St. Mary's, but I buried three persons at St. Clement's, where it broke out violently, and the vicar had left Oxford. It was a relief to me when Newman returned. I preached on 1 Pet. iv. 19,[1] which sermon Newman said was a comfort to him ; and I got safely to my friends in Wales, whom I had almost despaired of seeing again. On returning to Oxford at the end of that Long Vacation (1832), Newman said that he was afraid he should be treating me very hardly, but he had a plan of leaving me with St. Mary's entirely on my hands, and going

[1] "Wherefore let them that suffer according to the will of God commit the keeping of their souls to Him in well-doing, as unto a faithful Creator."

abroad with Froude, who had appearances
of incipient consumption about him. All
this was to me a great undertaking; for,
in addition to the tutorship in college, I
was also to be the Dean for the ensuing
year. However, it was so agreed, and
they were to sail with Archdeacon Froude
at the end of the year. Before parting
with Newman, I showed him my little
green book of English verses, sonnets,
etc., which I had written at Bisley and
which Froude had mentioned to him. He
told me he was, of course, delighted with
them, but said they were too soft (perhaps
he may have said effeminate); but, however, they were at the time the occasion
of kindling in himself the flame. And he
wrote some little poem daily, which he
sent home to us in letters, composed on
board of ship or otherwise on his travels.
His mother and two sisters were then

I

living in a cottage by Littlemore, called Rose Hill, and I saw them very constantly in the care of the parish, and in consequence of hearing his letters to them read to me, I have not by me so many letters from him, as I participated in his letters to his family at the time. All these poems have since appeared in the " Lyra Apostolica." I have mentioned that they were sent home to us at that time in his letters.

I may here add that there was one exception to this, in that most beautiful little poem, " Lead, kindly Light, amid the encircling gloom." This I saw for the first time in the *British Magazine,* and said to Newman, " Whose poem is that ? John Keble's, is it not ? It is not like you ; but if it is yours I will tell you when it was written. It was when you were coming home ill." He answered, " You are quite right. It was on board

the vessel from Sicily, when I was just
recovering, and very weak." And this
accounts for a tone in that poem which is
unlike Newman, more subdued and touching. But yet I have heard it noticed by
Copeland that it ends unlike the resignation of the Psalmist in Ps. xliii.

At this time, while Newman was abroad,
his brother Frank also was away in the
East, having gone on a wild, enthusiastic
expedition to Bagdad ; and when his
family were receiving or expecting letters
from both brothers I was struck with the
contrast between the two. While our
Newman, the eldest, had so much poetry, ✓
love of scenery and associations of place
and country, and domestic and filial affection, these qualities appeared to me wanting in his brother, who would have passed
by Jerusalem and Nazareth without turn-
ing aside to look on them, or the most

beautiful object in nature, or, at all events, would not deign to mention them nor to cast any longing, lingering look to his home. I notice this contrast the rather because time has since shown the same basis of constitutional character in both, so much so, that while pursuing opposite courses, they seem one and the same as if two ships were started on a voyage round the world in opposite directions and both split at last upon the same rock.[1] The domestic and poetic and social element in our Newman's character

[1] *December* 8, 1859.—In Dr. Moberly's book on "The Love of God" the two Newmans are compared together, and as a Fellow of Balliol he had opportunities of knowing Frank Newman, no doubt, and Froude also, who slightly knew Frank Newman, and had the greatest admiration for his talents, in mathematics especially; yet I cannot but think that the differences between the two brothers were very great and important. It is remarkable that one family should have had two such brothers as John and Frank Newman; and another family Hurrell Froude and his brother Anthony.—(Author's note.)

appeared to me providentially intended to
correct that constitutional restlessness of
intellect, that want of balance and repose
in the soul, which appears the malady of
both brothers. But our Newman, partly
from circumstances, and partly under the
false guise of mortification, has stifled those
his domestic affections, thereby greatly
increasing this his intellectual malady ;
whereas I never thought so highly of him,
and he never seemed to me, so saintlike
and high in his character as when he was
with his mother and sisters. `The softness
and repose of his character then came out,
and so corrected that restless intellect to
which he has been a prey.[1] For his temp-

[1] *December* 8, 1859.—I was making these same
remarks to Bishop Forbes last summer at Pusey's at
Christ Church. He seemed much struck with it, but
I think Pusey did not *quite* assent. However, this in
no way changed my conviction. Bishop Forbes was
mentioning that a friend of his had been lately with

tations were peculiar and of a high and spiritual nature, so that what would have been a course of self-denying discipline to others was not so to him. But these reflections are anticipating the course of this narrative. My own feelings on their absence are expressed in a sonnet in the " Thoughts in Past Years," " Behind are Ocean's Gates," etc.

Froude and his father returned to England, and left Newman, who was bent on seeing Sicily, and the circumstance which I most remember about that time was a conversation with Froude which was the first commencement of " the

Newman at the Oratory at Egbaston, and was giving a curious account of his life ; but what struck me was, how like Newman it all was, though the Bishop did not know this ; I mean Newman's living with persons younger than himself, a party reflecting his own opinions, his constraint in public, his entirely throwing it off with friends in private afterwards.—(Author's note.)

Tracts for the Times." He returned full of energy and of a prospect of doing something for the Church, and we walked in the Trinity College Gardens and discussed the subject. He said in his manner, " Isaac, we must make a row in the world. Why should we not ? Only consider what the Peculiars, *i.e.* the Evangelicals have done with a few half truths to work upon ! And with our principles, if we set resolutely to work, we can do the same."[1] I said " I have no doubt we can make a noise, and may get people to join us, but shall we make them really better Christians ? If they take up our principles in a hollow way as the Peculiars (this was a name Froude had given the Low Church party) have done theirs, what good shall we do ? " To this Froude said, " Church

[1] All this I have since expressed in a poem in the " Thoughts in Past Years."—(Author's note.)

principles, forced on people's notice, must work for good. However, we must try; and Newman and I are determined to set to work as soon as he returns, and you must join with us. We must have short tracts, and letters in the *British Magazine*, and verses, and these you can do for us— and get people to preach sermons on the Apostolical Succession and the like. And let us come and see old Palmer (*i.e.* the author of the 'Origines Liturgicæ'), and get him to do something." We then called on Palmer, who was one of the very few in Oxford—indeed the only one at that time—who sympathized with us, and, although he did not altogether understand Froude, or our ways and views—the less so as he was not himself an Oxford, but a Dublin man—yet he was extremely hearty in the cause; looking more to external, visible union and strength than we did, for we only had at heart certain principles. We, *i.e.* Froude, Keble, and myself, immediately began to send some verses to the *British Magazine*, since published as the " Lyra Apostolica." This, indeed, Newman did not like, when he returned, for he wished to have had throughout the management. I also, the same summer, sent to the *British Magazine* translations from the Parisian Breviary which I had by me. Mr. Rose,[1] who conducted that magazine, I liked, and respected extremely, but never saw him but once or twice. We were very few then in number, and any communication to the *British Magazine*, in favour of Church principles, was at once identified with their author, although anonymous.

---

[1] Hugh James Rose, Rector of Hadleigh, Essex ;— a good and wise man, who took a great interest in the Church Movement from the beginning, although himself a Cambridge man.—(Editor.)

K

The Long Vacation had commenced, and Newman had not only not returned, but his letters, which before had been very frequent, had for some time suddenly ceased. Day passed after day, and week after week, and his mother, sisters, and myself, daily looked on each other with blank dismay, when at last a line came, saying he had been very ill, but was better, and was returning from Sicily. He had been taken by the fever of the country, with no friend near ; and had proceeded some way, feeling very ill, but refreshed (he said) by fields of camomile, which he afterwards found was used as the great remedy for that fever of the country. Although his life was in imminent danger, yet, he said, he was sustained by a strong feeling on his mind, which never left him, that he should be spared to work out the conceptions he had formed for the Church. Such an idea would, of itself, have much assisted a recovery even as a natural cause. It was then, on returning from Sicily in a very feeble state, that he wrote those verses '' Lead, kindly Light," etc. From this time forth, after Newman's return, I was thrown more and more entirely into his society for about seven years, Froude waning more and more away, and disappearing from Oxford, being obliged to go to Barbadoes for a milder climate. The poems (since published as the " Lyra Apostolica ") appeared monthly in the *British Magazine;* and in addition to those which I contributed to it, I also continued to send some of my own to the *British Magazine,* together with translations from the breviary, and occasional letters. When, after the poems contained under that head had appeared in the

British Magazine, Newman published the
" Lyra Apostolica," he got Samuel Wilberforce—now the Bishop of Oxford—to
review it, as one who would do it in
a popular manner. Newman was then
much annoyed with the reflections of
the review on himself—and this was the
cause, I consider, of his never writing a
verse afterwards.[1] Indeed, I have heard
Miss Keble observe that it appeared to
have stopped in Newman what Providence
seemed to have designed as a natural vent
to ardent and strong feelings ; whereas
had it not met with that untimely dis-
couragement he would probably have
continued to write poetry, as he had then
begun, to the profit of himself and us all.

[1] This was written in 1851. I do not know
whether Newman wrote any more poetry before
Isaac Williams's death, in 1865, but we all know that
he did write poetry of very great power afterwards,
especially the " Dream of Gerontius."—(Editor.)

For, she said, her brother would never
have written verses were it not for the
encouragement he met with in his own
family. Samuel Wilberforce was not much
acquainted with Newman, though proud
of knowing so remarkable a person.[1]   I

[1] *December* 4, 1859.—The Bishop of Oxford seems
wonderfully improved* in depth and reality of character
of late, his alienation from Court, the troubles of his
office, his family trials and afflictions, his nearest
relations dropping off to the Church of Rome, his
intimacy with Prevost, his acquaintance at one time
with Copeland, who had the curacy of Garsington,—
all these things seemed to have worked upon him for
good. And, indeed, even in his brother Robert
Wilberforce, the Archdeacon, I observed something of
a similar change before he joined the Church of
Rome. Religion and religious principle appeared
in him more and more real than they used to do
at one time. Allowances must be made for a certain
hereditary Wilberforce character, but they were very
estimable persons. The younger brother, Henry, was
(as Froude used to express it) "caught younger." He

* I am persuaded that had the author lived to see
the support given by Bishop Wilberforce to Bishop
Gray, he would have expressed himself much more
decidedly.—(Editor.)

had up to this time no acquaintance with Pusey, but he would (now that we had lost Froude from Oxford) join Newman and myself in our walks. They had been Fellows of Oriel together, and Newman was the senior. But Pusey's presence always checked his lighter and un-restrained mood; and I was myself silenced by so awful a person. Yet I always found in him something most con-genial to myself—a nameless something which was wanting even in Newman and, I might almost add, even in Keble. But Pusey at this time was not one of us, and I have some recollection of a con-

was a college pupil of Newman's, and looked up to him with something of an idolatrous veneration. The Bishop of Oxford said, in this room, " I often told Henry that he was not himself when with Newman. He loses himself and his own mind." Yet a little while before Henry joined the Church of Rome, Newman said to him, " My temptation is to Scepti-cism," a very remarkable confession, which the Bishop mentioned to me.—(Author's note.)

versation which was the occasion of his
joining us. He said, smiling to Newman
and wrapping his gown around him, as
he used to do, " I think you are too hard
upon ' the Peculiars ' as you call them (*i.e.*
the Low Church party) ; you should con-
ciliate them. I am thinking of writing
a letter myself with that purpose," or
rather I think it was of printing a letter
which had been the result of private correspondence. " Well," said Newman,
" suppose you let us have it for one
of the Tracts?" ". Oh no," said Pusey,
" I will not be one of you." This was
said in a playful manner, and before we
parted Newman said, " Suppose you let
us have that letter of yours, which you
intend writing, and attach your own name
or signature to it ? You would then not
be mixed up with us, or be in any way
responsible for the Tracts." " Well,"

Pusey said, at last, "if you will let me do that, I will." It was this circumstance of Pusey attaching his initials to that tract, that furnished the *Record* newspaper and the low Church party with his name, which they at once attached to us all. And indeed that conciliating tract on Baptism seemed to aggravate them more than the rest. Thus the circumstance of Pusey's wishing to stand aloof from us, as a party, served to connect him ever afterwards most intimately with us, as if he were the head of the party.

Mrs. Pusey was alive at that time, and I liked her also, which was an additional bond between us, but I have no recollection of anything then moved between us on Church matters. They once asked me to dine with them alone, when by some mistake I did not go ; and at another time I remember a large party at dinner there,

where was Dr. Hook and a great many
Churchmen. I remember, too, Mrs. Pusey
coming to me at Mrs. Newman's funeral,
when I read the service over her in St.
Mary's, at which we were all much affected.
Mrs. Newman's death was rather sudden ;
she was taken ill on the day of her
daughter's marriage. Poor Newman was
very much overcome by it, he seemed so
much attached to her and his sisters, and
leaned entirely on myself, clinging to my
arm at the funeral in great distress. In
the depth of his affliction he said, "I
have very much to tell you, but I cannot
now. Some other time." But he never
recurred to the subject.[1] His mother, a

---

[1] I have found amongst the author's papers the
following letter, evidently written by him just at this
very time :—

"MY DEAREST NEWMAN,

"I am vexed at being obliged to go away
on these days, when I might have seen a little of you.

L

little time before, had taken great interest in the building of the church at Little-more, for which reason Newman put up a monument to her in that church. It was considered quite a model of a church at the time, though built hastily. Oak-

This sermon * was a comfort to me at the time I heard it, so I send it in case it might be so to any of you. I hope, my dear N., we may all be able to raise our minds to think of these our friends as something better than their poor remains, and for our own re-grets for what we wish might have been different, may we not find a cure in the † πάντοτε ὑπὲρ πάντων εὐχαριστεῖτε (which I think is given us more than once), ἐν Κυρίῳ ἡμῶν Ἰησοῦ Χριστῷ.

"Believe me, with best affection,

"ISAAC WILLIAMS."

---

* The sermon is Thomas Keble's, and the text John xvi. 32. I have added it as an appendix, because it appears to me to exhibit simply and beautifully that calm sense of duty and humble peaceful resignation, which Isaac Williams so much admired and loved in T. Keble, and which deeply influenced his own character and teaching, as appears very plainly, I might almost say, throughout this autobiography.—(Editor's note.)

† Eph. v. 20 ; 1 Thess. v. 18.

ridge Church, in Bisley parish, which was being built at the same time, with so much more caution and care, was comparatively a failure. So much was it Newman's way to do things quickly and successfully. I was appointed the curate of Littlemore, and as we had the daily service there every afternoon, it was the constant walk of Newman and myself. I had lodgings there and spent the Sundays and Saints' days at Littlemore.

Thomas Keble had resolved, about 1816, when he made that collection of "Authorities for the use of the Daily Service" published in the "Tracts for the Times," that, if he ever had a parish of his own, he would at once begin daily service, which he did immediately on coming to reside at Bisley in 1827.

This was the origin of the revival of the daily service. The Kebles at Fairford were in the habit of reading the daily Church service in their family; and when Thomas Keble (in the year 1827) had the living of Bisley given him, then in lieu of the prayer-meetings which had been customary in that parish, he established the daily service in the church, which was then spoken of as a strange fancy. Having been therefore long accustomed to this, when I first became Newman's curate at St. Mary's, in common with a great many less definite opinions and practices which I imported from Bisley, one was a daily morning service at St. Mary's, to which we afterwards added this service at Littlemore in the afternoon, so that there should be both services daily in the parish.[1] It was from this that the custom has since prevailed throughout the kingdom.[2] I may mention

[1] See " Thoughts in Past Years."
[2] It had become nearly extinct, especially in

a little trifle which indicated the manner in which many more important matters owed their origin to Bisley. Our friend, Dr. Ogle, once wishing to designate our party, said, "You that read in church with a little book, I don't know what to call you." In asking him to explain the little book, I found what he meant was this: Thomas Keble at Bisley had used a little prayer-book at the daily service, in order to save the large parish book from being worn out by this his crotchet (as it was thought) of the daily service. Finding this little book convenient for my short sight, I did the same at St. Mary's, and Newman and John Keble finding it con- venient for the same reason, fell also into the custom of using one; and what New- man did was copied a little later than this

country parishes, though it did survive in a few places, even in the country.—(Editor.)

period by a host of young admirers. This, with a fast reading of the service[1] and other points, was copied from him. It was in this manner that many things at first owed their origin to Bisley in the way of Christian principles, of which I mentioned Newman's first volume of sermons as an example. For some time I had entire sympathy with Newman; he came to hold all the opinions I had been long used to, only in his expression of them going beyond what I myself should have done, writing of Saint Charles and George the Good. I think the last point into which we came in perfect unison of feeling was that of King Charles, that point which of all others I have always felt most deeply. But I remember New-man, even so late as my publishing the

[1] But this was not a custom either at Bisley or Hursley.—(Editor.)

Sonnet, now in "The Cathedral," on Charles the First, made an alteration which I have never quite liked, inserting the line,

" Flouted his name, unpardoned e'en in death,"

for one of mine which expressed more strongly my own feeling, but which I have never since remembered.

Copeland[1] had now come to reside in college at Trinity, about two years after I had done, and was to me an invaluable support; he was better acquainted with our English divines than anybody I ever met with, more especially the Non-jurors. And in addition to all this, he had been used to parochial work, without which no one can be more than half a divine. We worked together as well as we could to

---

[1] William John Copeland, Fellow of Trinity College, Oxford ;—from first to last united with Isaac Williams in the most intimate affection.—(Editor).

improve the college, but it was very up-
hill work. Short, who had been tutor for
six years before I had entered as an undergraduate, was the chief tutor still, and
though very good-natured and kind, seemed
almost incapable of looking on college
matters in a moral or religious light.
Even at that time I remember Newman,
who had been his pupil at Trinity College
as well as myself, saying of him, " Lusisti
satis, edisti satis atque bibisti, Tempus
abire tibi est." Expensive parties, too,
still continued, especially among the Heads
of Houses, who used to eat and drink
very freely, and therefore with them our
principles made us very unpopular ; and
Newman was very sensitive of ill-treatment, as he was susceptible of kindness.
But a marked change was now taking
place in the whole character of the University. College chapel was less looked

upon as a mere roll-call, or like appearing on parade in the army, to which tutors had before likened it. Fridays in Lent were still the chief days for party-giving with the heads of houses, but the younger members of the University were much changed ; many did not dine in Hall on Fridays—I had myself never done so, ever since I had been elected fellow—and much less wine was drunk in common room except by the seniors.

All the circumstances which were now taking place indicated the silent progress of the movement. When the Tracts were first published little or no notice was taken of them. I remember asking my pupil, Nevile, as he went home for the vacation, to call at booksellers' shops in large towns, and to inquire for the Tracts and to ask them to procure them ; I did so myself. But by degrees

M

Newman, when I daily went to his rooms after my lecture, would have some little incident to mention which implied that the movement was not dead. Then I remember his finding, to his great delight, an allusion to the Tracts in the *Times* newspaper.

I much regretted not being with poor Froude at or nearly before his death. He had much wished me to come to him, but I did not like leaving Norman Hill that Christmas,[1] where my mother was staying with the Prevosts, and we had not recovered the death of my second brother, Jonathan. My youngest brother, Charles, had been taken ill with a fever the year before, and died very suddenly at Cwm. He had been the strongest and finest-looking of the family, and at his death he had said, " My brother

[1] 1835.

Jonathan will not survive this "—almost the only thing he said. And it was very true, for, though endeavouring to bear up, yet being not at all strong before, and leaning much on Charles, he pined away and sunk. He died about a year afterwards. In consequence, I did not go to Froude that Christmas vacation. But Rogers did. Poor Froude! he was peculiarly *vir paucorum hominum.* I thought that, knowing him, I better understood Shakespeare's " Hamlet." Froude was a person most natural, but so original as to be unlike any one else, hiding depth of delicate thought in apparent extravagancies. " Hamlet " and the " Georgics " of Virgil, he used to say, he should have bound together. Many have imagined, and Newman endeavoured to persuade himself, that if Froude had lived he would have joined the Church of Rome as well as himself. But this I do not at all think.[1] There was a seriousness and steadfastness at the bottom in Froude so that I had always confidence in him.

Newman told me once, half seriously and half playfully, that the publication of " Froude's Remains " was owing to me, as I had said to him, if persons could have so much brought before them that they could thoroughly understand Froude's character, then they might enter into his sayings, but unless they knew him as we did, they could not understand them. For indeed one constantly trembled for him in mixed society—both in Common Rooms and in other places—feeling that he would not be understood. With

---

[1] *December* 9, 1859.—I find that John Keble and others quite agree with me that there was that in Hurrell Froude that he could not have joined the Church of Rome.—(Author's note.)

regard to the publishing, I always said
that I had faith in what was done by
Keble with Newman from the best of
motives, and doing violence to his own
feelings ; but I had never sanctioned
the publication or taken part in it. On
the day of the book coming out, I
went into Parker the bookseller's with
Copeland, and there we were startled at
seeing one who then was the chief oppo-
nent of Church principles of Newman
and ourselves. It was Ward, of Balliol,
author of the " Ideal." He sat down
with the book in his hands, evidently
much affected ; and then we afterwards
heard, to our astonishment, that he had
been very much taken by the book, had
bought a copy for himself, and another to
give away, and was, in fact, quite converted.
He was followed by his friend Oakeley, of
Balliol, who publicly in a pamphlet an-

nounced his adhesion, and privately also. Oakeley had always been a friend of Froude and myself, since we were under-graduates together. But he had been a pupil of Bishop Sumner, of Winchester, and latterly had taken up Erastian notions, but used often of late to ask me to ride with him and talk on Church matters. His abilities were rather showy, from an elegant pleasing style, than either acute or deep. He came afterwards to ask my opinion about his taking Margaret Street Chapel, in London, and I thought the Chapel was a sphere best suited for him, and where he might do us much good —his choice being between that and a college living, of which he had then the option. And he took the Chapel on my advice. Little did I foresee the issue and the change that was to come; but I represented to him that his abilities suited

him well for stating our views and principles in London; whereas, indeed, his
physical deficiencies, for he was lame,
rendered him less fit for a country parish.
Nor could he understand the country poor.
He was a very amiable person, but more
and more, from that time, carried away
to the Church of Rome, chiefly, I believe,
owing to some London influences. But
with him went Ward and Capes. It is
curious that Capes, about a year after
publishing a very juvenile book against
Newman, himself became quite a convert.
He came to Oxford, and Ward asked
Newman and myself to meet him in his
rooms at breakfast. I was disappointed
in not finding Newman there, but he told
me he had declined, as he could not meet
Capes till he had publicly cancelled his
book. This I understood Capes said he
could not do, as he had sold it to a book-

seller. However, this juvenile attempt Parker the bookseller had shown me at first, and I told him that it would be well to inform the author, through some friend older than himself, that he did not at all understand the subject he had thus written about. Soon after the publication, he became aware of this himself, but the book was referred to by the Bishop of Chester (now the Archbishop[1]) as the best refutation of the Tractarians, while the author himself had seen the ignorance of his youthful work. But I am anticipating the course of my narrative.

Pusey was very much overcome by the loss of his wife, so much so as to move us all, and myself especially. From that time he gave up everything like dinnerparties ; and he was thrown more with us. At this time we were swelling into a large

[1] Sumner, Archbishop of Canterbury.

party, and Pusey formed a plan of our meeting every Friday evening at his house, and reading lectures on some point in Divinity. Some of the " Tracts for the Times" were written for that purpose. Such was my Tract No. 80. I had now been in the habit of reading Origen's " Commentaries on the Gospels," and there observed how much he alluded to a mysterious holding back of sacred truth, such as I had always been struck with in the conduct of the Kebles. And this view was much confirmed by my own studies connected with our college lectures on the Gospels, which led me constantly to notice this in our Lord's conduct. At Norman Hill,[1] in the vacation, I wrote out these thoughts in an essay; showed it to John Keble, who wished it to be one

[1] Then Sir G. Prevost's residence in Gloucestershire. —(Editor's note.)

N

of the Tracts, and I read it at Pusey's on a Friday. When talking of it there, with Newman and Pusey, the former suggested that he should attach to it the name of " Reserve in Religious Teaching." I mention this circumstance because some were more alarmed at the name than anything else. Yet, as Bishop Thirlwall of St. David's very kindly observed respecting it, " The very title, ' Reserve *in* Teaching,' intimated that the teaching of the Gospel was not withheld, for it was '*in* teaching it' that the caution was to be exercised." This, I think, he mentioned in a Charge ; and he mentioned to me privately that the Bishops of Winchester[1] and Gloucester[2] evidently misunderstood it. The latter, indeed, could not have understood it if he had read it, for he did not understand ethical and religious subjects of that

[1] Bishop Sumner.   [2] Bishop Monk.

nature; but he took his notion of it, I believe, from the newspapers. Having been in the habit at that time of occasionally meeting him, I took him greatly by surprise when I wrote and told him that the tract was mine. With regard to the great obloquy it occasioned from the Low Church Party, this was to be expected—it was against their hollow mode of proceeding; it was understood as it was meant, and of this I do not complain. Some, again, among ourselves, hardly understood it, and, while objecting to it, spoke kindly of it and its author. Amongst these was Arthur Perceval. Some, again, were in some degree alarmed, and I think perhaps Newman himself made use of it to further his own secret inclinations towards the Church of Rome.

I afterwards wrote Tract No. 87 in explanation, which I believe quite did

away with all reasonable objections ex-
cepting those of the Low Church. But
the Bishop of Gloucester made a charge
against it in complete ignorance, thinking
it was Newman's, but not only not under-
standing, but apparently not having read
it, and, as it appears from a letter to me,
ignorant of the very existence of the latter
part of it, *i.e.* of No. 87. What I complain of in him is his not having acknowledged his error, when it was pointed out
to him. I am not aware of any one else
that I have to complain of with regard
to that Tract. It did its intended work,
and I was well content to bear with the
outcry and opposition.

With regard to my other Tract, No. 86,
on our own Prayer-book, the occasion of
it was this: I thought that Newman and
Keble, by their publication of " Froude's
Remains," appeared to be disparaging our

own Prayer-book, and I wrote this, as arguing with them on their own grounds. And when staying with John Keble at Hursley I showed him what I had written. He expressed the strongest concurrence and delight in it. This, I said, I did not expect from you, for it was written as against you. But he wrote to Newman saying we must have it for the Tracts for the Times. I explain this its origin and intention, as it might seem allowing too much to foreign churches, and claiming too little for our own ; but it was intended as an *argumentum ad hominem*, to correct what might appear to be going too far from our own Church in " Froude's Remains."

Another subject on which I put together my thoughts at this time was the Epistles of St. Paul, about which I wrote in an article for Newman in the *British Critic*, in a review on Mr. Forster's book, on the Epistle to the Hebrews. Newman also pressed me into an article on Keble's " Psalter," but I was not satisfied with my performance.

About the same time as the tract on " Reserve," I published " The Cathedral," in pursuance of the same great object we had undertaken, and after that the " Thoughts in Past Years," consisting mostly of poems, written long before " The Cathedral," and I always thought with more poetry in them. Many concurring circumstances had now tended to strengthen Church principles. The attempt of the Government to force the University to receive Dissenters, which was thrown back by the unanimous action of the whole body. I remember Denison, the present Bishop of Salisbury, meeting Newman in Parker the bookseller's shop, and saying,

" To make a stand against the Government by a handful of men here is absurd. What do they care for you ? They will only despise you." But the event was very different. At that time we were determined to go by faith and not mind the chance of failure, and the stand so gathered strength that we had a meeting of the University in Magdalen Common Room, with Burton, the Divinity Professor, in the chair, and a determination in favour of a strong simultaneous resistance became almost unanimous. I think there were but two dissentients, and they did ultimately sign our protest or appeal. Of these Jacobson, since the Divinity Professor, was one. And Oxford, from the strength of principles shown there, was becoming a rallying point for the whole kingdom. John Keble's assize sermon before the judges against the Latitudinarian government was thought indiscreet and fruitless. But these things were not so.

I watched from the beginning, and saw among ourselves greater dangers than those from without, which I attempted to obviate by publishing the "Plain Sermons." I attempted in vain to get the Kebles to publish, in order to keep pace with Newman, and so to maintain a more practical turn in the movement. I remember C. Cornish[1] coming to me and saying, as we walked in Trinity Gardens, " People are a little afraid of being carried away by Newman's brilliancy; they want more of the steady sobriety of the Kebles infused into the movement to keep us safe. We have so much sail, we want

---

[1] Charles L. Cornish, Fellow of Exeter College, a man on whose judgment Isaac Williams placed great reliance.—(Editor.)

ballast." And the effect of the "Plain Sermons" was at the time very quieting ; they soothed the alarms of many. Sewell made good use of them in a very telling article in the *Quarterly ;* Maitland, of Gloucester, said, "Well, there is surely no popery there." I thought of publishing these sermons, in connection with the Tracts, and with Newman's concurrence undertook it, being actuated with fears for the result of Newman's restless intellectual theories. I wrote the preface for those sermons, expressing my apprehensions ; but this advertisement was so altered at Bisley by Jeffreys [1] and others, as to have been quite spoilt, as things are which are written by one person and altered by others. I began at first with the Kebles, especially Thomas Keble

[1] Student of Christ Church, then Curate of Bisley, now Vicar of Hawkhurst, Hon. Canon of Canterbury.

O

of Bisley, whose sermons are so very simple and striking. Pusey was afterwards glad to afford me a whole year of his sermons. Newman said it would swamp my boat; but it was not so. It served my purpose. I joined Copeland with myself as joint-editor, who entered into my views. Newman afterwards, when I had left Oxford and lived at Bisley, wrote to say he should be glad to afford a year's sermons in the series. In this I acquiesced, and felt sure that he would fall in with my wishes, by sending the least controversial of his sermons; and so much was this the case, that I have thought they must have been some of his earliest written sermons, so quiet is their tone.

In first undertaking the publication of these " Plain Sermons," I had no encouragement from any one—not even from

John Keble. Acquiescence was all I could gain. But I have heard John Keble mention it as a saying of Judge Coleridge, long before the Tracts for the Times were thought of, " If you want to propagate your principles you should lend your sermons, the clergy would then preach them and adopt your opinions." Now this has been much the effect of publishing the " Plain Sermons." [1]

---

[1] *December* 13, 1859.—It was curious to observe the gradual accessions of strength and indications of progress in Oxford. There were here and there opponents changing their minds. Ward, who was always walking with Stanley, and apparently full of arguments against us, attended Newman's week-day lectures in St. Mary's ante-chapel to refute them ; preachers at St. Mary's were changing their tone, and especially preachers from the country coming up to attack us in the university pulpit, not at all knowing the subjects or our principles and views ; add to this persons coming to see us from Ireland and Scotland interested in our movement, but more especially from America —one a dissenting preacher and D.D., with whom Newman and Pusey were much taken, more than

Nothing had as yet impaired my friendship with Newman. We lived daily very

I was myself; his abhorrence of or popular shrinking
from the blacks made me distrust him from the first—
others good churchmen, as John Williams, and
afterwards Dr. Potter, who came to me at Bisley,
both since bishops, and other interesting Americans.
Copeland has never ceased to inveigh against the
Heads of Houses as the causes of so much mischief,
and indeed of all the evil that ensued by their irritating
opposition ; but I doubt whether harm was done by it.
Though disturbed of course by a self-denying religious
reformation, and jealous of the influence obtained by
it, yet notwithstanding, there were also in some cases
grounds for their distrust. But the condemnation
of Dr. Pusey's sermon by the six doctors (Hawkins,
Symons, Ogilvie, Jenkyns, Jelf, and Godfrey Faussett)
was very inexcusable ; it was the cause of my voting
against Symons's appointment as vice-chancellor.
Nemesis, however, came on them when Pusey at last
threw his broad shield of protection over them (to
save the annihilation of the hebdomadal board), by
a large vote of convocation against Gladstone and
the Government. But this was long after. One
curious instance of tergiversation in the opposite way
took place in our friend Golightly. He was strongly
with us, had taken a house in Oxford in which he
said he should hide us when persecution arose ; but
he soon himself became our chief persecutor.

much together; but I had a secret uneasiness, not from anything said or implied,
but from a want of repose about his character, that I thought he would start into
some line different from Keble and Pusey,
though I knew not in what direction it
would be. Often after walking together,
when leaving him, have I heard a deep
secret sigh which I could not interpret.
It seemed to speak of weariness of the
world, and of aspirations for something
he wished to do and had not yet done.
Of the putting out of Church principles

When on the point of becoming Newman's curate,
he preached a sermon in some church in Oxford
where Pusey was present, who (he told me) most
kindly wrote to him to point out all the mistakes
he had made in his sermon; Newman, on hearing
of this, said he could not be his curate, and from that
time even to this present day he lives in Oxford the
active watcher and accuser against Church principles,
and at present the accuser of Bishop Wilberforce of
Oxford.—(Author's note.)

he often spoke as of an experiment which he did not know whether the Church of England would bear, and knew not what would be the issue. The times one can look back upon as the brightest, were seasons of relaxation, as on Sunday evenings; for on Sundays we always dined together privately in each other's rooms with one or two friends. It is not merely, as on usual social meetings, that I look back on those occasions, but because such repose and relaxation seemed to me to bring out the higher and better parts of Newman's character. I allow that something sarcastic and a freedom of remark would blend with such unbendings, but it was better out in playfulness than fermenting within. But at all times there was a charm about his society which was very taking, and I do not wonder at those being carried away who had not been previously formed, like myself, in another, or at all events, an earlier school of faith. The first secret misgiving which arose into something of distrust was when two of Newman's pupils—S. Wood, since dead, and Robert Williams (M.P. for Dorchester)—were translating and on the point of publishing the Roman Breviary (with the hymns translated by Newman) without any omissions. On Prevost's earnestly deprecating this, a dispute ensued, and I thought Newman showed some want of meekness. This, and not his opinions, weakened in some slight degree my confidence; and in looking back, most intimately as I was united with him, I cannot remember when my prayer for him was not rather that he might be preserved from error and the dangers to which he was exposed from his peculiar temperament, than for his perfection, and that I might follow his example, as would have been my prayer with regard to John Keble and Pusey. But it is only on the retrospect one is sensible of this difference.

It is sometimes supposed that Newman's leaving the Church of England was owing to the ill-treatment we met with in consequence of our principles, especially from the Heads of Houses at Oxford. Certainly Newman was very sensitive of such things, more so than the rest of us, and I think I have heard even Pusey attribute his change to it. But I doubt it. I think it more owing to his own mind.[1] And what was

[1] I have heard Dr. Pusey speak of Newman as "forced out of the Church of England," and there can be no doubt, I should say, that the heads of houses adopted the line of conduct that was most calculated to goad a sensitive nature like Newman's to desperation. Nevertheless, I believe that Isaac Williams may be right in attributing his change *more* to what was working within him,—to his natural restless temperament.—(Editor.)

most important, he had the countenance
of a most judicious and kind bishop, in
Bishop Bagot, then Bishop of Oxford.
The first circumstance that indicated this
was very early—the first thing that brought
Newman's name before the public. There
was a pastry-cook in St. Mary's parish of
the name of Jubber. Newman, on going
abroad with Froude, had told me that he
had in vain endeavoured to get that family
baptized. The son had wished me to bap-
tize him, but I found it was entirely from
secular motives, to obtain a certificate.
While I was still engaged in this matter,
Newman returned, and soon after, one of
the daughters wished to be married. This,
as she persisted in continuing unbaptized,
Newman refused to do.   On this the
newspapers made a violent outcry against
him, and the old-fashioned orthodox shook
their heads. Newman wrote to the bishop,

P

saying, if he desired him, he would marry them, and he was a little annoyed at receiving no answer. But in the midst of this, Newman was appointed to preach the visitation sermon at St. Mary's; and the bishop, though he never alluded to the subject, showed him the most marked attention and kindness, which, I thought, indicated his respect for him before the clergy.

Not very long after, Newman and myself went to Bisley outside the carriage of John Keble and his wife, who had been lately married. This was the only time that Newman was at Bisley. The bishop was there for a confirmation. Newman was then more in sympathy with the Church of England than at any time, and he was introduced to the Bishop of Gloucester as the author of the "Arians." But he expressed to me his disgust at so luxurious a dinner prepared for a bishop. It would be better at such a time, he said, that a bishop should only ask for a little dry bread and salt and water. These things, and the great annoyance he always felt at John Keble's marriage, indicated feelings not at all in unison with the established state of things in the Church of England. And indeed some time afterwards, when Prevost[1] was asked by Dr. Inglis, Bishop of Nova Scotia, to be made Bishop of New Brunswick, the acceptance of which would have been a great self-denial, Newman said, " I don't know how he could accept such an appointment under any circumstances from the State. I could not."

[1] It seems right to say that, though I did decline the proposal of Bishop Inglis to go out as a missionary, with the prospect of being afterwards bishop, it was not from any objection to a nomination by the Crown, but on account of my wife's very delicate health.—(Editor.)

Many have naturally supposed that it was the condemnation of the Tract No. 90, by the Heads of Houses, which gave his sensitive mind the decided turn to the Church of Rome. But I remember circumstances which indicated it was not so. He talked to me of writing a tract on the Thirty-nine Articles, and at the same time said things in favour of the Church of Rome, which quite startled and alarmed me, and I was afraid he would express the same in this tract, with no idea (as his manner was) of the sensation it would occasion. After endeavouring to dissuade him from it, I said, " Well, at all events let me see it first." On returning after the vacation, he said, " I have written that tract after all, but you have no need to be alarmed, for I have got John Keble to look it over, and he says nothing against it." Very true ; but he had not the reasons for apprehension that I had. Yet, still, the sensation and the strong and bitter opposition it excited seemed to take Newman quite by surprise. I remember well being with him when Ward came into his room, on the day of its publication, and said, " There is an immense demand for that tract, and it is creating a tremendous stir, I find from Parker's shop." Newman walked with me at the time of the con- demnation of it, much depressed. And he wrote to apologize for it to Dr. Jelf, partly unsaying it. This also was his manner ; he was carried away first of all by his own mind, but afterwards, from a very amiable and good feeling, wished to do away with the uneasiness occasioned. But his decided leaning to Rome came out to me in private, before that tract was written. Certainly he felt neglected before by the University, and constantly

irritated by the Head of his college ; and
I used to be surprised he had not more
learned to look on persecution as a matter
of course, what a good man must expect
to meet with, and which should be to him
a satisfaction, as indicating him to be in
the way of truth. Yet nothing had as yet
impaired our intimacy and friendship,
until one evening,[1] when alone in his rooms,
he told me he thought the Church of
Rome was right, and we were wrong, so
much so, that we ought to join it. To
this I said that if our own Church improved, as we hoped, and the Church of
Rome also would reform itself, it seemed
to hold out the prospect of reunion. And
then everything seemed favourably pro-
gressing beyond what we could have dared
to hope in the awakening of religion,

[1] This conversation took place *after* the publication
of Tract No. 90.—(Editor.)

and reformation among ourselves. That
mutual repentance must, by God's blessing, tend to mutual restoration and union.
" No," he said, " St. Augustine would not
allow of this argument, as regarded the
Donatists. You must come out and be
separate." This conversation grieved and
amazed me, and I at once wrote and gave
Newman to understand that we could not
be together so much as we had been. I
owed it to myself. I had no right to put
myself into temptation; to subject myself
willingly to influences which must operate
so powerfully on the mind (for what could
be more attractive than such influence ?),
and thus to be led to what I was now
assured was wrong. Yet still nothing of
the nature of ill-will or a quarrel arose
between us. But he was extremely
annoyed at " The Baptistery," when it first
came out, from my speaking so much

against the Church of Rome in it, and a
few words passed between us.   It was one
Sunday morning, when there was a great
fire in the High Street.   But he immediately afterwards wrote to me very kindly,
and in great distress.

It was a great relief to me at that time,
when I knew not how far our mutual
friends agreed with Newman, that John
Bowden—Newman's oldest and best friend
—took me aside and thanked me greatly
for the way I had spoken in "The
Baptistery," against Rome, saying that
Oxford, which had always been before his
most delightful retreat, was now becoming
painful to him from the Romanizing
tendencies in some of our friends.   Yet
still, all this was long before it was publicly
known what Newman's thoughts really
were ; and he was for some time accused
by some of dishonesty and duplicity.   But

the fact really was, that he was wavering
very much in his own mind; and the feelings and thoughts he would express to one
person or at one time, differed very much
in consequence from what he might express
to another or on another occasion. And
I heard of his saying, " My old friends are
what I like, their ἦθος and character," mentioning myself and another—C. Cornish;
" but I like the opinions of my new friends,
though not themselves "—meaning especially Ward of Balliol. So slowly and
unwillingly did he put off his connection
with us. But I was, notwithstanding all;
one of the last to think that he would
really join the Church of Rome, because
I thought he would not submit himself to
any system. But when Thomas Keble
said in answer to this, "A man may do
and think as he likes in the Church of
Rome," I answered, " If this is the case,

Q

it will of course be different." Others, who first received the impulse from himself, served afterwards to draw him on. Yet he spoke of many who, for intellectual reasons, had resolved to join the Church of Rome, but were unaccountably held back by something which might be, he said, the Spirit of God. Yet, if this were the case, this suggestion might, as all other warnings of the Good Spirit, be stifled and quenched by acting contrary to them. And it was after this time that at Oakeley's suggestion, I understood, he used the prayers to the Virgin in the Breviary, which he had not done at first, and this is often the strong overt act towards joining that communion. Yet still, I said to myself, if this be the leading of the Good Spirit into another Church, we shall see the fruits of it, or hear of them in holiness of life. But that the reverse has been

the case has been throughout too evident,
and that the characters of those who have
gone from us have not improved by the
change. The person to whom Newman
most deferred had been Froude, though
younger than himself. But I think even
his influence would not have stayed Newman's restless mind.

With regard to John Keble. I asked
him at this time to come up and preach
at St. Mary's on St. Andrew's Day, when
I got a turn for him, in order to check the
disloyal, unquiet spirits that were rising
up. He came and preached, but he said
he found it exceedingly difficult, as it made
known to others the distrust we had of
some among ourselves—and for this reason
he did not preach the sermon he intended,
but another—both, I think, since published.
In Keble's judgment and steadfastness I
always had the greatest confidence ; but

as every one has his weak side, so his is this—that from his love and partiality to his friends, especially if they are at all persecuted, he has been apt to be so taken with their opinions, that from his humility he will often apparently adopt them for his own. So that when I say that his opinion has of all the greatest weight with me, yet I am obliged to ask whether it is *his own* opinion (from what I well know of him) or only that of others. Thus I have heard him hold even with Oakeley and Ward, and he defended the translation of Bonaventura by the former because he said it did him good. "Now," I said, "I remember how strongly you condemned this in the Calvinists, when they said their hymns do them good; so (you said) might an Ode of Pindar do me good, but it is not therefore Scriptural truth. Yet now you use this very argument yourself for

these things in another direction." And
a conversation of this kind gave rise to the
"Lyra Innocentium," for Keble said he
thought of altering the "Christian Year" to
adapt it to his present views. "Well," I
said, "if you do, we have the former, and
we will ourselves reprint it and keep to it.
If you want to express your altered views,
write another book, and then we can still
keep to the old." About the same time,
on looking at John Edward, his godson,
then an infant,[1] he said, "Why should
there not be a future 'Cathedral' in him?
Think of this. Does not the idea inspire
you to write a book of poems about it?"
These thoughts and conversations at
Bisley, after we had settled there, gave
rise to the "Lyra Innocentium." But I do
not mean to say that there ever was any
real difference of opinion between John

[1] Isaac Williams' own child.—(Editor.)

Keble and myself, it was only that when Newman and others were in their transition state, and before they left, John Keble, for love's sake, held with them; and I wished always to show that it was himself, his own former self, that was to be trusted, and that these notions did not belong to him. And as soon as they had left us, it was otherwise. " Now that I have thrown off Newman's yoke," said he one day to me, "these things appear to me quite different." [1] Nor has anything occa-

[1] *December* 6, 1859.—About a year ago, when staying at Hursley, I remember John Keble saying, " I look now upon my time with Newman and Pusey as a sort of parenthesis in my life; and I have now returned again to my old views such as I had before. At the time of the great Oxford movement, when I used to go up to you at Oxford, Pusey and Newman were full of the wonderful progress and success of the movement—whereas I had always been taught that the truth *must* be unpopular and despised, and to make confession for it was all that one could do; but I see that I was fairly carried off my legs by the sanguine views they held, and the effects that were showing themselves in all quarters."—(Author's note.)

sioned more defections to the Church of Rome than that many persons adopted opinions and principles which Newman latterly put forth, while he appeared to be with us, which necessarily led to the Roman Church, and which he held as holding with the Church of Rome, without sufficiently considering what those principles were, and to what they led. It was very long before men were able to recover themselves sufficiently to reconsider their views and judge for themselves, free from Newman's influence.

December 7, 1859.—It seems to be a popular notion that the original writers of the Tracts have generally joined the Church of Rome, and that therefore that movement of itself has been so far a failure ; but this is very far from being the case, for it is a very remarkable circumstance, and one which I find very much

strikes every one to whom I have mentioned it, that out of all the writers in the
" Tracts for the Times," one only has joined
the Church of Rome. And another remarkable fact is that whereas those writers
are sometimes popularly said to have been
originally of the Evangelical school, the
only one, I believe, who was so, was this
very one who has joined the Roman
Church. From which it appears that there
is standing ground in the Church of
England between these two extremes.
Of all who took any part, however slight
and trivial, in the " Tracts for the Times,"
I can make out fourteen, and I do not
think there were any more—Froude, Newman, John and Thomas Keble, Arthur
Perceval, John Bowden, Isaac Williams,
Pusey, Benjamin Harrison (since Archdeacon), William Palmer (author of the
" Origines Liturgicæ"), Thomas Mozley,

Sir George Prevost, Antony Buller, and R. F. Wilson.

Another circumstance which occurs to me is this, that while such a vast number of persons have joined the Church of Rome in consequence of Newman's influence (for indeed almost all the secessions are in some way or other traceable to that influence either immediately or in its effects), yet these seceders were persons who looked upon him at a slight distance, or mixed with him on feelings of inferiority as younger or less intimate, and especially such as "sat under him," to use a popular sectarian expression, such as Oakeley, Manning, Ward, Faber, and perhaps a hundred or more of others. Nothing can exceed the excessive interest with which many of these have inquired of me respecting all his sayings and doings. But what is most striking, there does not appear to

R

have been any who associated with Newman on terms of equality, either from age, or position, or daily habitual intercourse, or the like, in unrestrained familiar knowledge, who have followed his example in seceding to the Roman Church, such, I mean, as Fellows of Oriel, who lived with him (and some of them friends in the same staircase), as Rogers, Marriott, Church, the two Mozleys (his brothers-in-law), John Bowden, Copeland, J. F. Christie, Pusey, the Kebles.

When Sir Frederic Rogers[1] was staying here a year and a half ago, I had some very interesting conversations with him on these subjects. He said that he very much wished he could have broken off from Newman in the way that I did, during the latter part of Newman's stay among us, for it was a very painful time

[1] Afterwards Lord Blachford.

to him, and has left a very uncomfortable retrospect; for seeing him daily as a Fellow, living in the same staircase, and having been in the habit of living with him, he entered into constant controversies and disputations with him, which produced at length a sore and irritable feeling, so that there ceased at last to be any friendliness between them, in that his separation from us.

On the contrary I am able to look back with feelings of great thankfulness that during that very critical period of Newman's gradual withdrawing from us, when he shut himself up in his monastery at Littlemore, and previously during the latter part of his stay at Oxford, I was able to withdraw myself from him, and that too with mutual good feeling, and indeed during the last part of this interval I had left Oxford for Bisley and was married.[1] Whereas, with Copeland it was just the contrary; he began to be thrown more into the society of Newman, as I withdrew myself from it, and this especially from his taking the curacy of Littlemore, just as Newman went to reside there. The consequences of this have been to him exceedingly trying. He could not, I think, ever have joined the Roman Church as his brother has done. But his mind and body were all but overwhelmed with the great trial, distress, and perplexity, out of which he was a long time before he recovered; for Newman's words during all that time sank very deeply within him, so impressive and penetrating were his sayings. Newman's saying to him with surprise, "Could you sign the Thirty-nine Articles? I could

[1] Married Caroline, third daughter of Arthur Champernowne, Esq., of Dartington, at Bisley, 1842.

not!" made him for some time incapable
of doing so, or taking a living or any
charge that required it.   And to this
day Copeland has Newman and his
sayings always in his mind.

LETTERS FROM NEWMAN.

THE following letters from Cardinal Newman [1] are here inserted by the Editor, as showing at once Isaac Williams's unshaken and ever increasing faithfulness towards our own Church, and at the same time the tender regard and affection that subsisted between them to the last, and which we humbly trust is renewed in them now in the light of God's pure and perfect truth.

No. 1.

Littlemore,
October 8, 1845.

MY VERY DEAR WILLIAMS,

I do not like not to send you just a line, though I know how it will

[1] I have to thank the cardinal's executor, Father

distress you. Father Dominic, the Passionist, is coming here to-night on his way to Belgium. He does not know of my intentions, but I shall ask of him the charitable work of admitting me to what I believe to be the one true fold of the Redeemer. He is full of love for religious men among us, and believes many to be inwardly knit to the Catholic Church who are outwardly separate from it. This will not go till all is over. You may suppose how much Bisley has been in my thoughts lately.

This is a short letter, but I have a great many to write.

Ever yours affectionately,
J. H. N.

No. 2.

Abbotsford, Melrose,
December 21, 1852.

MY DEAR WILLIAMS,

I received your affectionate letter here last night, and thank you for

Neville, for his kindness in giving me permission to publish these letters.

it with all my heart. I am banished from home at this season on account of my health, and, if I must be an exile, I cannot have a pleasanter place of banishment or kinder hosts than the present inmates of Abbotsford. I have nothing definite the matter with me ; but the incessant stress of twenty years on my brain and nerves have brought, what medical men call, my " vital powers " very low. My only symptom is excessive weakness. When I was finishing the " Arians," at the beginning of the period I speak of, I was daily, if not fainting away, yet feeling as if I were, and such effects of mental application are not likely to be less now. So the doctors have decided I must do nothing; and I have promised to do nothing till Easter.

We have been building a large house at Birmingham during the last two years, and all the time it was building I kept saying, " We shall have some cross, mark me !" And certainly such a shower has come upon us as to be like nothing else than meteoric stones from heaven, through the last year, so much so that we almost fear to build our church, lest a more grievous fall of the like loving chastisements should come on us. Certainly, personally speaking, I never have, through my life, had such a year as the last, and it is a wonder I have got through it as I have.

You only say the truth when you anticipate I remember you tenderly in my prayers, though you are, my dear Williams, if you will let me say it (in answer to what you say yourself) of "the straitest sect,"and, as a matter of duty, will not let heaven smile upon you. But it is so difficult to say a word without wounding most tender feelings, that, though I should not have spoken on the subject, if you had not, yet pray give me your pardon, as you read, if this sentence is needlessly painful to you.

Ah! if I had any portion of St. Paul's true zeal in my heart, I should have some portion of gentleness in my words.

Ever yours, my dearest Williams,
Most lovingly and affectionately,
JOHN H. NEWMAN.

S

No. 3.

The Oratory, Birmingham,
June 7, 1863.

MY DEAREST ISAAC,

Your letter came an hour or two
ago. I rejoiced to have it. Is it possible
you should not have seen more of Oxford
of late years than I have? I have not
seen more than its spires in passing since
February 22, 1846. I dined and slept at
dear Johnson's, and left for good. I only
heard lately that the cap and gown had
gone out, and yet did not believe it, till
you have confirmed it. *Heu quantum
mutatus ab illo!* Of all human things
perhaps Oxford is nearest my heart,—and
some parsonages in the country. I cannot
ever realize to myself that I shall never
see what I love so much again, though I
have had time enough to do so in. But
why should I wish to see what is no
longer what I loved? All things change ;
the past never returns here. My friends,

I confess, have *not* been kind—I suppose
this is what you allude to, as my having
expressed it to Copeland. But, really, I
think I have a reason. I should not here
notice it, if *you* had not. If they act *on
principle*, I should not say a word, but
love them the better for it. If they said,
as we used to say of Arnold, "I cannot
recognize you," I understand it fully and
am satisfied. But such cases are the
exception. * * * Well, if I spoke severely
to Copeland, I am sorry for it,—but I
don't think I did. I am *not* "holy," in
spite of you, but I think I *am* "calm and
loving," though I wish there were more of
supernatural grace and holiness in that
calm and love. But to return. If any
place in England will right itself, it is
Oxford: but I despond about the cause of
dogmatic truth in England altogether.
Who can tell what is before us? The
difficulty is that the arguments of infidelity
are deeper than those of Protestantism,
and in the same direction. (I am using
Protestantism in the sense in which you

and Pusey would agree in using it.) And how can you back to something more primitive, more Christian, a whole nation, a whole Church ? The course of everything is onwards, not backwards. Till Phaeton runs through his day, and is chucked from his chariot, you cannot look for the new morning. Everything I hear makes me fear that latitudinarian opinions are spreading furiously in the Church of England. I grieve deeply at it. The Anglican Church has been a most useful breakwater against scepticism. The time might come when you as well as I might expect that it would be said above, " Why cumbereth it the ground ? " but at present it upholds far more truth in England than any other form of religion would, and than the Catholic Roman Church could. But what I fear is that it is *tending* to a powerful establishment teaching direct error, and more powerful than it ever has been ; thrice powerful, because it does teach error. It is what the Whig party have been at all our time, not destroying the

establishment, but corrupting it. Do
you recollect little John Whitman? He
is now a man of thirty and a shoemaker,
living near us. He was calling on me an
hour ago. He has just lost his mother.
She broke a leg and died. She and
Whitman live in St. Clement's, he tells
me. He is a nice fellow, but I neither
liked, nor now like, father and mother,
poor things. He was brought up by Mrs.
Small and Mrs. Tombs, and never lived
at home.

Ever yours affectionately,

JOHN H. NEWMAN.

No. 4.

The Oratory, Birmingham,
March 31, 1865.

MY DEAREST ISAAC,

All last summer I was trying to
get to you—but really I am tied by the
leg here. In November I got away to
the Sussex coast for a week—else, I was
here almost through the whole year.
Copeland's account has saddened me very

much—and I had been anxious before it. I don't forget, but remember with much gratitude, how for twenty years you are perhaps the only one of my old friends who has never lost sight of me—but by letters, or messages, or inquiries, have ever kept up the memory of past and happy days. How mysterious it is that the holiest ties are snapped and cast to the winds by the holiest promptings—and that they who would fain live together in a covenant of gospel peace, hear each of them a voice and a contrary voice, calling on them to break it! I cannot stir till Easter—but then I should like of all things to run down to you.

 . Ever yours most affectionately,

JOHN H. NEWMAN.

The Rev. Isaac Williams.

No. 5.

The Oratory, Birmingham,
May 4, 1865.

MY DEAR SIR GEORGE,

I have been planning another visit to dear Isaac, and your letter comes.

My first sad thought is that in a certain sense I have killed him. I am sure so it is, that he did not rally after driving me down to the station. He has really been a victim of his old love for me. He has never lost sight of me—ever inquiring about me from others, sending messages, or writing to me. I so much feared he was overdoing himself—but he would not allow it. I wanted him to let me walk down, but he wanted to have more talk; and then, when he set off, he could not say a word. But it is all well; and God knows better than we do. I am most glad to have seen him, though I have (as it were) killed him with a kiss. Well, I have sent him out of a world in which he had no part, except as far as it contained souls, with whom he was so lovingly bound up. Poor John Keble, how will it be broken to him?

When I first saw him on my arrival, I thought death was marked upon his face. But then I knew how strange his health had been for years; and, when he began to talk, he was so much himself, and his mind so clear, that the impression went. Well, I shall say Mass (if all is well) on Saturday for his dear soul; and so will Mr. St. John. May God wash it white in His most precious blood, and receive it into that eternal peace and light which it coveted above all things.

Very sincerely yours,

JOHN H. NEWMAN.

The Rev. Sir George Prevost, Bart.

P.S.—I have written a line to Mrs. Williams and I enclose it—asking you to take the trouble to read it, and to let her have it or not, as you think best.

POETRY PROFESSORSHIP.

December 9, 1859.—In looking back on those eventful times, there appear more distinctly in memory certain great occasions which brought out some crisis and marked the progress of persons and things; of these the last and crowning one was the contest for the poetry professorship in 1841–42. I had never sought or obtained any kind of University favour or office either of honour or distinction, except the Latin verse prize ; but it was looked upon as a matter of course by many that I should succeed Keble as Poetry Professor. Of itself I had neither time nor desire for it ; but my determination was fixed from

T

this circumstance. Piers Claughton (now the Colonial Bishop) came to me and asked me not to stand for the professorship, in order that his brother—the vicar, now of Kidderminster [1] — might stand, as two could not be candidates from the same college (and his brother was also of Trinity), grounding his application on the threat held out by some that I should be opposed as the writer of Tract No. 80 and for my church principles. I immediately said, "On this threat I cannot retire." Garbett was afterwards put up by the Principal of Brasenose with the prospect that a religious commotion might be excited. At first, things went on silently and quietly, without any overt act that stamped it as a religious or party movement. But this comparative quietude was very soon broken up by

[1] Afterwards Bishop of St. Albans.—(Editor's note.)

Pusey, unwittingly, and as it was thought most unwisely, for what he did immediately gave our adversaries all that they desired. This was a printed circular which he issued in my praise and in my favour, complaining of my being opposed merely and avowedly for my church principles, on the Head of Brasenose's own admission. Upon this the opposite party had promises pouring in on all sides, and many, who had been with us, held aloof, and some withdrew their promises. A regular reign of terror set in. The commotion filled the papers and all parts of the land, and many found their own secular interests would be seriously endangered by adhering to us. Some of these cases much distressed me. That the Low Church party as a body should all oppose me, as Wadham College did, was all right and natural—my Tract No. 80 was against them—they rightly understood it, there was no mistake ; but with others nearer home it was different. I will mention three cases. There was Boyle,[1] of Oriel, he wrote to say that, much as he had felt personally with me, as an old friend, he must go up from Scotland to vote against me as he was so opposed to us in principle, being himself in opinion, if not altogether, Presbyterian. This was all honourable and straightforward. I could not complain. But my excellent friend and companion, Ben Harrison, himself a writer in the Tracts, had now gone to be the Archbishop's private chaplain, and if he had written to say to me that in consequence of his connection with the Archbishop he could not vote for me, I should not have taken it

[1] Patrick Boyle, father of the present Earl of Glasgow. I remember that Boyle told me that he was married by a Presbyterian minister, no doubt of the established kirk.—(Editor.)

amiss. But he wrote to say that in consequence of an article of Ward's in the
British Critic, he could no longer identify
himself with us, by voting for me (his
most intimate friend). This vexed me,
for he knew well that I myself denounced
and disapproved of the article he spoke of,
more strongly even than he did. But,
after all, it was but this his *manner* of
holding aloof that I complain of. It was
my fault, I ought to have made more
allowances for him. His position es-
tranged him from us all, for a time. His
mind has now given way.[1] I have always
loved and valued him very much indeed.
The most trying case to me was that of
Bishop Wilberforce (not then Bishop of
Oxford). He had always been in familiar
intercourse with me—asking me for my

---

[1] He recovered, however, his powers of mind many
years before his death.—(Editor.)

new books, getting me to introduce Newman to him in every way. On receiving
the college circular he wrote to our
President, expressing his great interest in
the election, as I was his old and intimate
friend ; but some one observed at the time,
" Don't you notice how cautiously throughout he abstains from giving his promise ? "
And so, no sooner did it become the
unpopular side, than he took part against
me. Still I feel, on the retrospect, that
great allowances are to be made even for
this. The only thing I felt was that those
who knew well my opinions and agreed
with them, ought to have continued with
me. Other opponents were all fair and of
a different kind—many because I was
Newman's friend, and Newman was dis-
trusted at this time, and the new persons
he was getting about him, as Ward of
Balliol, were but half and hollow friends.

Others, again, as the heads of houses generally, were hostile to the whole movement. Thus a man in Wales, to whom my brother applied for his vote for me, said he should certainly vote against me, as he understood things were "come to such a sad pass in Oxford, that a man could not get a mutton-chop for supper." What he meant was that the supper-parties and potations had gone out under our influence.

It was indeed an exceedingly stirring time, and in the interval came the Christmas Vacation in the midst of the excitement. The new Bishop of St. David's, Bishop Thirlwall, on whom we had looked with such aversion, that some of us had seriously thought of contending against the confirmation of his election, from what we indistinctly heard of him, yet was found unexpectedly my friend, from a love of fairness and unbiassed spirit of inquiry.

He offered to come and consecrate the new church of Llangorwen[1] in Welsh with Bishop Andrews's service ; asked me particularly to preach the sermon, and afterwards to publish it, was personally very kind to me, and told me that the other bishops had not understood, some had not read, what I had written.

After this, a very large party, with Gladstone, my supporter, among them, and the Bishop of Oxford, *i.e.* Bishop Bagot, our friend, signed a requisition to both parties to retire. On seeing this, I immediately wrote a very long letter (which John Keble strongly approved), addressed to the Bishop of Oxford, stating the reasons that had constrained me to stand ; and that from my committee I had very

---

[1] Built and endowed by Isaac Williams's eldest brother, close to their old home at Cwmcynfelin, in this Bishop's diocese.—(Editor.)

sanguine reasons of success; but that I was but too glad to comply with the wishes expressed by my bishop in any way, and that, therefore, I at once withdrew and resigned the contest. Before, however, sending this letter to Bishop Bagot, it was necessary to lay it before my President and my committee; but the President of Trinity, Ingram, was of all things most jealous of interference from the Bishop of Oxford in any university affairs. Newman acquiesced in what I proposed to do, saying that our opponents, availing themselves of our episcopal obedience, were "*seething the kid in its mother's milk.*" In the mean time, before I had thus resigned at our bishop's wish, an agreement was made for a comparison of votes. They had a large majority. And immediately after its being made known, it was announced that the head of the opposite party, Dr. Gilbert,

the Principal of Brasenose, was made
Bishop of Chichester by Sir Robert Peel.
Dr. Gilbert had indeed become the head
of the anti-tractarian party at the time,
but in some degree accidentally, and not
altogether owing to difference in principle. When Newman went abroad in
1832–33, and left me in charge of St.
Mary's, Dr. Gilbert and Mrs. Gilbert were
very kind to me, and admired Newman
very much. Mrs. Gilbert told me long
after, that Dr. Gilbert always bought her,
as his own present, every book that
Newman wrote ; but he afterwards took
offence, chiefly from things said in the St.
Mary's pulpit, offensive and extravagant,
especially by Morris (Jack Morris, as he
was called). The Principal was an extremely irritable person, and became very
hostile to Newman, and in consequence,
when the contest for this election took

place, took a very active lead against us. But, after all, his opposition was mainly personal, as against Newman's friend, rather than grounded on a great antagonism of principles.

The Bishop of Gloucester did not behave kindly, or as it seemed to me fairly, at this election; he had in ignorance condemned my tract on "Reserve," in a Charge, and now, when people had become sensitive about obedience to bishops, some of my friends (Sewell, I think, was one) objected to my tract, not in itself, but as being under quasi-episcopal censure. On this, I published the Bishop's remarks in parallel columns with extracts from my tracts alluded to, showing that they were quite opposite to what the Bishop supposed. I wrote to him, and it became reported and publicly stated that he had withdrawn his censures; just at last I had a letter from him, long mislaid and misdirected to me at Trinity College, *Cambridge*, allowing that he knew not of the existence of the latter tract of mine on the subject of "Reserve" in the "Tracts for the Times" (and I believe he had not read the former). And then, at last, when it was too late for me to reply, he published a letter in the papers, saying that he did not retract his former censures, and so joined openly the popular party and Lord Shaftesbury, thus seriously influencing an Oxford University election, being himself a Cambridge man, and what he did and said told against me chiefly on account of that respect for a bishop's authority which we, the Tractarians, had always laboured to increase. But, however, I was glad afterwards to have made friends with him, and to have seen him in this house.

HIS DANGEROUS ILLNESS.

EXTRACT from a letter from the Rev. R. Suckling to the Rev. W. Scudamore, dated Kemerton Rectory, January 19, 1846:—

Of Isaac Williams's illness you have seen a notice. It is very serious. He is in a far advanced decline, and is not expected to live much beyond a month. He is in the house of his brother-in-law, Sir George Prevost.[1]

A friend of his was staying here last week (Mr. Christie) who had just seen him—taken his farewell leave of him—he

[1] At Stinchcombe, in the county and diocese of Gloucester, the parish of which I then was and still am the incumbent. A house was afterwards built for him, very near mine, where he lived seventeen years, and where he died May 1, 1865.—(Editor.)

describes him as most calm. His faith in our Church (he says) is most firm.

Dr. Pusey and many others have been to see him—but Archdeacon Manning's parting was very affecting—he kissed his hand and begged his prayers hereafter, when he should be in bliss—for himself and for our afflicted Church.

As the illness to which the above letter refers, and the recovery from it, were amongst the most remarkable events in Isaac Williams's life, it seemed to me right to insert it, the more so as we find it in the same manuscript book as the auto-biography, in his widow's handwriting. Isaac Williams survived to be Robert Suckling's biographer. I earnestly wish that life was still read, as it was for some little time after Suckling's very early death. It would (I cannot but think) help in leading the men of the present generation to look upon Christianity, not so much as a battle-field for contro-versialists, still less as a subject of com-promise, but as a matter intensely practical, founded on faith in the great verities of revelation—verities to be simply defended and maintained without wavering, but ever as *speaking the truth in love,* and as putting forth the strongest motives for tenderness and compassion for souls in misery and danger.

This illness began in the latter part of the year 1845, with a lumbar abscess, which physicians and surgeons considered most serious, but when that was healed, disease in the lungs came on, and in fact all the symptoms of rapid consumption. Certainly, in my long experience, I never saw a case in which the symptoms of that fatal complaint appeared to be more clearly or more fully developed. The expectoration, the night perspirations, the emaciation, were quite such as one is used to see, when consumption has reached its last stage. A physician from London came down to see him, and on his return told a friend of mine who was travelling with him, that life could not hold out more than five days longer.

We were all of us (relatives and friends) of course earnestly praying for him, but we had no hope of his recovery, nor had he himself. However, a doctor from Aberystwith, near his old home, tried some medicine that had not yet been tried upon him, and by God's marvellous blessing on the use of it, contrary to all expectation, he recovered, and his life was lengthened (though with weakened health) for nineteen years. I remember hearing a gentleman ask one of the doctors who had watched the case, whether it would not be well to put an account of a case so remarkable in some medical book. But the reply was, " I do not think we can attribute the recovery to any particular medical treatment. It was more the work of nature and Providence." His birthday was the 12th of December, and, according to the Lectionary then in use, the thirty-eighth chapter of Isaiah was read at Evensong, which records the lengthening of the days of Hezekiah, and this he and his friends often mentioned. The latter years of his life, after this illness, were spent in retirement, but yet in constant occupation, for some time partly in the education of his sons, but throughout the whole period in writing sacred poems, and in the composition of sermons and commentaries on Holy Scripture. I knew a good man, well acquainted with Dr. Pusey, who being asked by a bishop

x

whether he thought Pusey would follow Newman, replied " I cannot think it ; he *lives* in the Scriptures." It was the same reverential love for his Bible, the same *life* in it, that sheltered Isaac Williams to the end alike from Romanism and from Rationalism.

CONDEMNATION OF DR. PUSEY'S SERMON.

THE following observations on the trial (if it can be so called) and the condemnation, by the six doctors, of Dr. Pusey's great sermon on the Eucharist, are found in Isaac Williams's own handwriting, at the end of the autobiography; as though he wished his children to know the true history of that sad business, and the feelings that it excited at Oxford. There is no doubt that Isaac Williams was the author of the paper, and the editor, in determining to publish it, has been fortified by the opinion of some of those who remembered those days, and in particular by that of him who has written the only history we have yet of the Oxford Movement.

Probable Effects of late Proceedings at Oxford.

Nothing has occurred in our time so pregnant with great consequences as the late conspiracy in Oxford. A barrier has given way, as in the march of revolutionary measures, when the divinity that hedges round the person of a king has been broken through. The first overt act never stops; so is it with our natural reverence for a holy person, when under any violent impulse this sacred feeling is trampled on, and God's withholding hand is withdrawn, it may be augured to be the prelude of great events. Certainly nothing has been known in our days like the feeling with which it has been received by all within the more immediate circles of Oxford society; men look at each other as if some wicked thing had been perpetrated on which they could not venture to speak ; in all there is a deep feeling that it is not to end here. And a sense of love and reverence for the injured person strongly entertained, but never perhaps before fully known or expressed, breaks out in sayings from men of all opinions, which have much struck me.

"He is so marked by the hand of Heaven, by sacred sorrows, and in every way" said one, "there is something so sacrosanct about him, that they dare not touch him ; it cannot be." "Why, he is like a guardian angel to the place," said another. "One feels as if one's own mother had been insulted," says a third ; "it overwhelms one as something shocking." There is also a very general impression that the sermon itself is no more than a handle for a preconcerted measure, which is confirmed by the fact that they have resolutely refused to mention any one objectionable proposition in the sermon, or to state in what way it is discordant with the Church of England ; all whom I have met with considered the sermon very innocent and unexceptionable. Add to which the circumstance of a similar attack at the same time upon another, where, *the particular charge being specified*, it was at once found untenable and frivolous. * * * As the Vice-Chancellor has still some time to continue in office, it is to be hoped he will remember that, in times when party spirit runs high, men in prominent places, however amiable and right in their intentions, if they have not the firmness to abide by their own opinions, become the worst of instruments in the hands of others, to hasten that crisis which they would be the first to deprecate. But what will Alma Mater do to clear herself? for such a spot on her fair name is not to be found. Setting aside the moral weight of Dr. Pusey's character, and that of his station as a canon of Christ Church, as a man of genius, neither the University or the nation have seen his superior for centuries. Add also that there is in the English character a strong sense against unfair dealing; persons in no way connected with this movement are loud against this proceeding. " I am no friend to them and to their views," said one man in my hearing, " but this is a sad business ; what will the world say of such a judge and jury ? "

Again, will it urge men to Rome ? This is the apprehension of many. I think not, for two reasons; first, that when a person feels that others have a desire to thrust him from his place, he becomes actuated by a double desire to retain it more fully and broadly, and a desire to urge the party to Rome is too evident. In the second place, Dr. Pusey himself is the one of all others least inclined to secede to Rome, and this late occurrence has not only combined and rivetted together the whole Catholic body in the English Church, but especially around himself, by a sympathy and affection brought out and strengthened to an inconceivable degree.

Now all these are elements, the working of which prognosticate their final success in the struggle. Add to which, beyond all, the strength which always has moved the world and shaken it to its centre—the strength of principle. " It is but little," says Aristotle, "in outward show, but in worth and power far surpasses all things." Truth, moreover, never has prevailed except when persecuted, and from the beginning to this day it is impossible to put your finger on any point in history when the truth appeared and was not persecuted, since the time of which it is said *"And wherefore slew he him ? Because his own works were evil and his brother's righteous."*[1] It has passed into a principle observed by the wise man, *" Let our strength be the law of justice.*[2] *He was made to reprove our thoughts. He is grievous unto us even to behold, for his life is not like other men's, his ways are of another fashion. * * * He abstaineth from our ways as from filthiness. Let us see if his words be true."*[3]

Again, time tells in their favour, the

---

[1] 1 John iii. 12.   [2] Wisdom ii. 11.
[3] *Ibid.*, verses 14–17.

rising generation are with them. If seven doctors will condemn them, yet take seven of your youngest masters of arts at a venture for your jury, and they will as certainly find an acquittal. But still for the time being on the other side there is power—worldly power—those are known to be with them whose mere wishes are a law to some of a certain station and character. This implies a struggle, but nothing more; it is but as chaff before the wind before great principles.

(Signed) OXONIENSIS.

SERMON BY THOMAS KEBLE.

Ταῦτα λελάληκα ὑμῖν ἵνα ἐν ἐμοί εἰρήνην ἔχητε· ἐν τῷ κόσμῳ
θλίψιν ἕξετε· ἀλλὰ θαρσεῖτε· ἐγὼ νενίκηκα τὸν κόσμον.

"Hæc locutus sum vobis, ut in me pacem habeatis : in mundo
pressuram habebitis : sed confidite ; ego vici mundum."

"Hæc locutus sum vobis, ut in me pacem habeatis : in mundo
afflictionem habetis : sed bono animo sitis : ego vici mundum."

A Sermon of Thomas Keble's, sent by
Isaac Williams to J. H. Newman, no
doubt on the occasion of the Death
of Newman's Mother (see p. 73).

ST. JOHN XVI. 33.

"These things I have spoken unto you,
That in Me ye might have peace.
In the world ye shall have tribulation :
But be of good cheer ;
I have overcome the world."

THESE are the concluding words of our blessed Master's memorable address to His disciples, just before His last sufferings—a part of Gospel history to which our attention has this day been especially called. Throughout this touching address or conversation, there is nothing more worthy of the devout attention of all sincere Christians than the wonderful tenderness and compassion displayed by the adorable

Jesus towards the erring and afflicted, such as His disciples then were—*erring* in their notions about the nature of Christian earthly blessings ; and *afflicted* at the thought that those blessings would not be of the kind they had expected, especially that they could not much longer hope to be favoured with the visible presence of their Lord, but must be left, as they imagined, "orphans," and "comfortless" in the midst of a cruel world.

We first, then, observe how gently and tenderly, as His manner was, the holy Jesus rebuked them for their mistaken or imperfect notions of the nature and value of Christian privileges and blessings.

(And it may be worth while to recollect that this conversation took place either at the paschal table, immediately after they had eaten the Passover together, or else on the way as they walked from

Jerusalem to the garden of Gethsemane. Probably to the end of the fourteenth chapter as they sat at the table, the fifteenth and sixteenth chapters as they walked along.)

Thus, then, it was. Although our Lord had frequently foretold His own death and sufferings, yet the Apostles could not endure to hear of it or believe it. At length, when the time really approached, they began to be perplexed and alarmed, and put different questions to Him, such as their fears suggested. And the particular circumstance which seems *first* to have decidedly roused their apprehensions was the solemn and affectionate address which He made to them, just after Judas had left the room. " My children," He said, "yet a little while I am with you. Ye shall seek Me, and as I said unto the Jews, Whither I go ye cannot come; so

now I say to you." Upon this the zealous
St. Peter immediately asks whither He
was going, implying that wherever it
might be, he at least would not leave
Him. " Lord, why cannot I follow Thee
now ? I will lay down my life for Thy
sake." The more cautious St. Thomas,
anxious to have his *reason* convinced, and,
as it might seem, vexed at not having the
whole matter clearly explained to him,
seems to speak rather in an upbraiding
tone—" Lord, we know not whither Thou
goest, and how can we know the way ?"
Another apostle, St. Philip, evidently
deeply pained, like St. Peter, at the
thought of being separated from their
beloved Master, asks for some visible
token of God's presence with them, and
then they would (he said) be contented.
" Lord," said he, "show us the Father, and
it sufficeth us." And then the holy Jesus,

having gone on to explain to them that it did not of necessity follow that, because He left the *world*, He should therefore leave *them*, St. Jude also anxiously questioned Him how this could possibly be. " Lord, how is it that Thou wilt manifest Thyself unto us, and not unto the world ? " plainly showing that he had not as yet any clear notion of the nature of the Messiah's kingdom, but supposed it would be in outward show and splendour, like the kingdoms of this world, or, at all events, that its King, Christ Jesus, would remain personally and visibly on earth to protect His servants and to rule His Church.

Now we observe with what tenderness and gentleness the holy Jesus bore with this ignorance and (in some instances) hastiness and waywardness of His chosen Apostles, or, as He called them, friends,

z

and how gradually, yet significantly, He brought the truth before them. *They* were thinking of a great kingdom, and themselves to be the chief persons in it. *He* washes their feet as a slave, and then says, " I have given you an example : " " The servant is not greater than his lord."

They were expecting a great kingdom, speedily to be established by Him, such as should be the wonder and admiration of the world. *He* plainly told them, " Yet a little while, and the world seeth Me *no more.*"

They were looking for high honours and places in the new kingdom. He told them to expect nothing from the world but " hatred," and " persecution," and " death," exactly as Himself had received from it. " If the world hate you," said He, what then ? "ye know that it hated Me before it hated you." " If they have persecuted Me, they will also persecute you." " The time cometh, that whoso-ever killeth you will think that he doeth God service."

Thus decisively, and in language of which the meaning could not be mis-taken, did our Lord put an end to any hopes which His disciples might have cherished of any mere *earthly* honours or success, attending the faithful profession of His Gospel ; thus tenderly, yet earnestly, did He labour to convince them that all their notions of His king-dom, as being like the kingdoms of this world, were erroneous, and could only lead to disappointment.

Yet, at the same time, it is also most worthy of our observation with what gentleness and infinite compassion He regarded their condition, cast down as they then were with the thought of being

separated from their beloved Master, and
with the evil prospect which lay before
them of the treatment they were to expect after He was gone from a cruel, or,
at best, an unfeeling world.

Thus sometimes He begs them, as it
were, to turn their thoughts to the *miracles*,
which He had now for three years past
been working in their presence ; and they
must confess that they might as reasonably
become atheists, and deny the providence
of God altogether, as distrust the power
and love of Him their Saviour. " Let
not your heart be troubled : ye believe
in God, believe also in Me." And afterwards, to one of the Apostles especially,
who begged for some strong overpowering
evidence of God's presence with Him,
that so there might be no longer any
room for doubt or misgiving, our Lord's
argument was of the same kind, after His

tender condescending manner, "Have I been so long time with you, and yet hast thou not known Me, Philip? He that hath seen Me hath seen the Father; and how sayest thou then, Show us the Father. . . . Believe Me that I am in the Father, and the Father in Me: or else believe Me for the very works' sake."

In which our blessed Master seems to have encouraged in His sorrowing disciples both then and in every age, the disposition so pathetically set forth in the exquisitely beautiful one hundred and forty-third Psalm.

"My spirit is overwhelmed within me [says the
     psalmist];
My heart within me is desolate.
I remember the days of old;
I meditate on *all Thy works;*
I muse on the *work of Thy hands.*"[1]

For here, you observe, He points out

[1] Ps. cxliii. 4, 5 (Bible Version).

the only refuge for an overwhelmed spirit and a desolate heart, to be in remembering, meditating, and musing on God's works— His works of nature and of providence possibly *He* might mean—but *we* can look to much greater works, His works of grace.

Nor need we look far without finding. For as every leaf and flower shows the hand of God in what we call the natural world, so does every page of Scripture, the history also of nations and of individuals, contain evidences of His love and power in the world of grace ; so that to the Christian's eye, purified by faith, the works of God even in this dim world are ever presented, and he everywhere traces the hand of the great Workmaster, infinite power, and (if the expression may be allowed) more infinite love.

It might perhaps have been expected

beforehand that in our blessed Lord's discourse delivered to His Apostles, or, as He was pleased to term them "His friends," on so remarkable an occasion, and when He was so soon about to leave them, it might have been expected, I say, that He should have dwelt much or even chiefly on the happiness in store for the faithful in heaven, as a hope sufficient to counterbalance all their present sufferings.

Yet you may observe that on this occasion He who knew what was in man, said but little on this great and glorious subject. "I go to prepare a place for you. And if I go and prepare a place for you, I will come again, and receive you unto Myself; that where I am, there ye may be also."

And afterwards—"Ye shall be sorrowful, but your sorrow shall be turned into joy." . . . "I will see you again, and your heart shall rejoice, and your joy no man taketh from you."

These, I believe, are the only expressions in the whole of our Lord's discourse, which seem to turn the thoughts of His afflicted disciples to that subject, which one would have thought most suitable to supply them with consolation and encouragement under such trying circumstances—the thought, I mean, of their heavenly reward, in His eternal presence.

Yet this, you see, is not at all dwelt on or explained, and perhaps we may without presumption say, for this reason, because there is danger, if we suffer our imaginations to rest too much on that state of bliss, that kingdom prepared for God's blessed ones from the beginning of the world, there is a danger of our forgetting those daily duties assigned to each of us here in our respective stations, and by the neglect or fufilment of which (without reference to our hopes and feelings) we show ourselves faithful or unfaithful servants of our Redeemer and God.

In what way, then, it may be asked, did He offer comfort to them in their affliction ? For that they were deeply afflicted, and that one great, if not the principal, purpose of His discourse to them at that time was to offer to them substantial consolation, no attentive reader of this touching portion of the Gospel history can, I suppose, question or deny.

The answer must be, that he *set them to work* "to do their duty in that state of life to which it had pleased God to call them," as therein and therein only they would find substantial hope and comfort, having the promised aid and guidance of the Almighty Comforter, and united in-

visibly indeed and spiritually, yet sub-
stantially and really, to their beloved Lord
who was only gone, as He Himself assured
them, to prepare a place for them, and
would surely come again and receive them
to Himself, never more to be separated.

I say, that our blessed Master taught
His disciples to look for substantial comfort
under affliction in the diligent accomplish-
ment of their present high and sacred
duties, rather than in any less active
anticipations of the final reward, may
appear, as from the general tenor of these
divine discourses, so from express passages
therein—such, for instance, as these—

" If ye love Me [as ye profess to do,
then] keep My commandments, and I will
pray the Father, and He shall give you
another Comforter, who shall abide with
you for ever (*i.e.* during all the time of
your earthly trial), even the Spirit of

Truth." " He that hath My commandments and keepeth them, he it is that
[really] loveth Me, and such an one My
Father will love, and We will come unto
him and make Our abode with him." Oh,
words of solid, heavenly consolation!

And afterwards, " Herein is My Father
glorified, that ye bear *much fruit, so* [i.e.
in bearing much fruit] shall ye be My
disciples."

This, as to what they must *do*, and as
to what they must *suffer* or be prepared
to suffer; the same calm resolute persever-
ing disposition He intimated would be
required of them.

It was not, indeed, according to the
world's mode of administering consolation
to speak of the sufferings that awaited
them (" The time cometh that whosoever
killeth you, will think that he doeth God
service "), yet even thus did the Saviour

comfort *His* friends, that they might be
ready and prepared for whatever should
happen, or (in His own words), that when
the time should come, "they might remember that He had told them of these
things." "Ye shall be sorrowful" said He,
"but your sorrow shall be turned into joy."
"Ye now, *therefore* [i.e. as a matter of
course] have sorrow : but I will see you
again, and your heart shall rejoice, and
your joy no man taketh from you."

And closing all with those memorable
words of divine compassion and encouragement. "These things I have spoken unto
you, that in Me ye might have peace. In
the world ye shall have tribulation : but be
of good cheer ; I have overcome the
world."

Thus did He, our Lord and Saviour,
animate His chosen disciples and friends
to go on their way rejoicing, in every

way, whether in the way of doing or
suffering, to seek only their heavenly
Father's will, trusting to the aid of the
Eternal Spirit through life, and for final
acceptance, only to the blood of the ever-
lasting covenant.

Then, said He, though " in the world,"
i.e. in your frail condition as weak and
sinful mortals, "ye shall have tribulation,"
yet " be of good cheer; I have overcome
the world."

Now, to us these words are spoken no
doubt as much as to those who heard them
from the Saviour's lips.

We, if we are indeed sincere in our
Christian profession, we too must feel in
a manner separated and absent from our
heavenly Lord—in this world we must
" have tribulation."

And it is plain, from this discourse of
our Lord's, that what the lowly Psalmist

said long before of his own case, is what
all sincere lovers of the great and good
God, whether before or since the Christian
dispensation, will apply to themselves.
" It is good for me [he said] that I have
been afflicted." [1]   So plainly in this
divine discourse, comprehending as one
may almost say the dying words of the
Saviour, the not merely benefit, but the
absolute *necessity* of affliction in some
shape or other, to wean our hearts from
worldly affections, and to turn them to
God, is most energetically set forth.

But why the *necessity* of afflictions? it
may be asked.   To which the answer
seems to be, that without them it is scarce
possible for us to have that deep, solemn,
serious sense of the importance of true
religion, and of the effects of our present
behaviour on our condition in eternity.   I

[1] Ps. cxix. 71 (Bible Version).

say we need, the most of us, some very
solemn and striking warning to make us
feel these things as we ought.

We are too apt, the best of us, to go on
from day to day, as if we were sufficiently
secure of our spiritual interests, and then
we grow cold and slack in our devotion,
in our acknowledgment of the greatness
of our privileges, and the greatness too of
our danger.

And when these great matters are for-
gotten, or at least but faintly remembered
in the bustle of daily thoughts and
business, then the heart by degrees
becomes less open to a sense of the love
and mercies of our God and Redeemer,
and we make the attempt (alas! how
vainly) to "have peace" in worldly com-
forts and satisfactions, too much forgetting
our only, our Almighty Friend. Indeed,
He plainly tells us that "in Him we may

have peace," this peace He offers us if
only we will yield ourselves to His love
and service. Not that we are to expect
anything like freedom from afflictions, nay,
quite the contrary. " In the world ye
shall have tribulation." Peace in Christ
Jesus, and tribulation in the world go
together, you see, to make up the true
" Christian's destiny."

And then if we be *indeed* true Christians,
to us no doubt has been addressed the
gracious farewell encouragement of the
King of Martyrs. " Be of good cheer ;
I have overcome the world."

Nothing, then, remains, but that for the
little ·time longer we have to remain in
this world, we seek rest and peace only
in the love and service of our Lord and
Master.

Nor expect at all to have this peace
without tribulation, but rather receive

tribulation even thankfully as the seal and pledge of peace.

That in all our conduct, but especially in what we call our religion, we be very *sincere*, and full of awe, and quite in earnest, as remembering in Whose presence we are.

And, then, come what will, whether it be called good or evil, we shall by the aid of the heavenly Comforter, make it all good to us by receiving it calmly, manfully, and with true Christian presence of mind. And we shall be neither much elated when things seem to go well, nor much cast down when they seem to go ill, (and it is but a seeming either way), but be only praying and striving that we may every day be more and more worthy of our high title of Christians, and more disposed with all sincerity, and with filial reverential love, to bless our heavenly

2 B

Father's Name, "for all His servants departed this life in His faith and fear, only beseeching Him to give us grace so to follow their good examples that with them we may be partakers of His heavenly kingdom."

Now to God the Father, God the Son, etc.

THE END.

PRINTED BY WILLIAM CLOWES AND SONS, LIMITED,
LONDON AND BECCLES.

Works by Isaac Williams, B.D.

Late Fellow of Trinity College, Oxford.

A DEVOTIONAL COMMENTARY ON THE GOSPEL NARRATIVE.

Crown 8vo. 5s. each. *Sold separately.*

THOUGHTS ON THE STUDY OF THE HOLY GOSPELS.	OUR LORD'S MINISTRY (Second Year).
A HARMONY OF THE FOUR EVANGELISTS.	OUR LORD'S MINISTRY (Third Year).
THE HOLY WEEK.	OUR LORD'S PASSION.
OUR LORD'S NATIVITY.	OUR LORD'S RESURRECTION

FEMALE CHARACTERS OF HOLY SCRIPTURE.
Crown 8vo. 5s.

THE CHARACTERS OF THE OLD TESTAMENT.
Crown 8vo. 5s.

THE APOCALYPSE : with Notes and Reflections.
Crown 8vo. 5s.

SERMONS ON THE EPISTLES AND GOSPELS
for the Sundays and Holy Days throughout the Year.
Two Vols. Crown 8vo. 5s. each. *Sold separately.*

PLAIN SERMONS ON THE CATECHISM.
Two Vols. Crown 8vo. 5s. *Sold separately.*

SELECTIONS FROM THE WRITINGS OF ISAAC WILLIAMS, B.D. Crown 8vo. 3s. 6d.

TRACTS FOR THE TIMES.
PLAIN SERMONS. By Writers of " Tracts for the Times."
LYRA APOSTOLICA. New Edition. With red borders.
16mo. 2s. 6d.

[Poems by J. W. BOWDEN, R. H. FROUDE, J. KEBLE, J. H. NEWMAN, R. I. WILBERFORCE, and I. WILLIAMS ; with a New Preface by CARDINAL NEWMAN.]

LONGMANS : LONDON.

POETICAL WORKS.

Each volume uniform, 32mo, 2s. 6d.

THE CATHEDRAL ; or, The Catholic and Apostolic Church in England.	HYMNS TRANSLATED FROM THE PARISIAN BREVIARY.
THE BAPTISTERY ; or, The Way of Eternal Life.	THE CHRISTIAN SCHOLAR.
	THOUGHTS IN PAST YEARS.

The Small 8vo Editions of the following may also be had.

THE CATHEDRAL ; or, The Catholic and Apostolic Church in England. 5s.
THE BAPTISTERY. With Plates by BOETIUS A BOLSWERT. 7s. 6d.
THE CHRISTIAN SCHOLAR. 5s.
THE SEVEN DAYS OF THE CREATION. 3s. 6d.

PARKER : LONDON AND OXFORD.

A Catalogue of Works

IN

THEOLOGICAL LITERATURE

PUBLISHED BY

MESSRS. LONGMANS, GREEN, & CO.

39 PATERNOSTER ROW, LONDON, E.C.

Abbey and Overton.—THE ENGLISH CHURCH IN THE EIGHTEENTH CENTURY. By CHARLES J. ABBEY, M.A., Rector of Checkendon, Reading, and JOHN H. OVERTON, M.A., Rector of Epworth, Doncaster, Rural Dean of Isle of Axholme. *Crown 8vo.* 7s. 6d.

Adams.—SACRED ALLEGORIES. The Shadow of the Cross —The Distant Hills—The Old Man's Home—The King's Messengers. By the Rev. WILLIAM ADAMS, M.A. *Crown 8vo.* 3s. 6d.

> The Four Allegories may be had separately, with Illustrations. 16mo. 1s. each. *Also the Miniature Edition. Four Vols.* 32mo. 1s. each; in a box, 5s.

Aids to the Inner Life.

> Edited by the Rev. W. H. HUTCHINGS, M.A., Rector of Kirkby Misperton, Yorkshire. *Five Vols.* 32mo, cloth limp, 6d. each; or cloth extra, 1s. each. *Sold separately.*
> Also an Edition *with red borders*, 2s. each.

> OF THE IMITATION OF CHRIST. By THOMAS À KEMPIS. In Four Books.

> THE CHRISTIAN YEAR.

> THE DEVOUT LIFE. By ST. FRANCIS DE SALES.

> THE HIDDEN LIFE OF THE SOUL. From the French of JEAN NICOLAS GROU.

> THE SPIRITUAL COMBAT. By LAWRENCE SCUPOLI.

Bathe.—Works by the Rev. ANTHONY BATHE, M.A.

> A LENT WITH JESUS. A Plain Guide for Churchmen. Containing Readings for Lent and Easter Week, and on the Holy Eucharist. 32mo, 1s.; or in paper cover, 6d.

> WHAT I SHOULD BELIEVE. A Simple Manual of Self-Instruction for Church People. *Crown 8vo.* 3s. 6d.

Bickersteth.—Works by EDWARD HENRY BICKERSTETH, D.D., Bishop of Exeter.

THE LORD'S TABLE; or, Meditations on the Holy Communion Office in the Book of Common Prayer. *16mo. 1s. ; or cloth extra, 2s.*

YESTERDAY, TO-DAY, AND FOR EVER : a Poem in Twelve Books. *One Shilling Edition, 18mo. With red borders, 16mo, 2s. 6d. The Crown 8vo Edition (5s.) may still be had.*

Blunt.—Works by the Rev. JOHN HENRY BLUNT, D.D.

THE ANNOTATED BOOK OF COMMON PRAYER: Being an Historical, Ritual, and Theological Commentary on the Devotional System of the Church of England. Edited by the Rev. JOHN HENRY BLUNT, D.D. *4to. 21s.*

THE COMPENDIOUS EDITION OF THE ANNOTATED BOOK OF COMMON PRAYER: Forming a concise Commentary on the Devotional System of the Church of England. Edited by the Rev. JOHN HENRY BLUNT, D.D. *Crown 8vo. 10s. 6d.*

DICTIONARY OF DOCTRINAL AND HISTORICAL THEOLOGY. By various Writers. Edited by the Rev. JOHN HENRY BLUNT, D.D. *Imperial 8vo. 21s.*

DICTIONARY OF SECTS, HERESIES, ECCLESIASTICAL PARTIES AND SCHOOLS OF RELIGIOUS THOUGHT. By various Writers. Edited by the Rev. JOHN HENRY BLUNT, D.D. *Imperial 8vo. 21s.*

THE BOOK OF CHURCH LAW. Being an Exposition of the Legal Rights and Duties of the Parochial Clergy and the Laity of the Church of England. Revised by Sir WALTER G. F. PHILLIMORE, Bart., D.C.L. *Crown 8vo. 7s. 6d.*

A COMPANION TO THE BIBLE: Being a Plain Commentary on Scripture History, to the end of the Apostolic Age. *Two vols. small 8vo. Sold separately.*

THE OLD TESTAMENT. *3s. 6d.*   THE NEW TESTAMENT. *3s. 6d.*

HOUSEHOLD THEOLOGY : a Handbook of Religious Information respecting the Holy Bible, the Prayer Book, the Church, the Ministry, Divine Worship, the Creeds, etc. etc. *Paper cover, 16mo. 1s.* Also the Larger Edition, *3s. 6d.*

Body.—Works by the Rev. GEORGE BODY, D.D., Canon of Durham.

THE SCHOOL OF CALVARY ; or, Laws of Christian Life revealed from the Cross. A Course of Lectures delivered in substance at All Saints', Margaret Street. *Small 8vo. 3s. 6d.*

THE LIFE OF JUSTIFICATION : a Series of Lectures delivered in substance at All Saints', Margaret Street. *16mo. 2s. 6d.*

THE LIFE OF TEMPTATION : a Course of Lectures delivered in substance at St. Peter's, Eaton Square ; also at All Saints', Margaret Street. *16mo. 2s. 6d.*

Boultbee.—A COMMENTARY ON THE THIRTY-NINE ARTICLES OF THE CHURCH OF ENGLAND. By the Rev. T. P. BOULTBEE, formerly Principal of the London College of Divinity, St. John's Hall, Highbury. *Crown 8vo.* 6s.

Bright.—Works by WILLIAM BRIGHT, D.D., Canon of Christ Church, Oxford.

LESSONS FROM THE LIVES OF THREE GREAT FATHERS: St. Athanasius, St. Chrysostom, and St. Augustine. *Crown 8vo.* 6s.

THE INCARNATION AS A MOTIVE POWER. *Crown 8vo.* 6s.

FAITH AND LIFE : Readings for the greater Holy Days, and the Sundays from Advent to Trinity. Compiled from Ancient Writers. *Small 8vo.* 5s.

IONA AND OTHER VERSES. *Small 8vo.* 4s. 6d.

HYMNS AND OTHER VERSES. *Small 8vo.* 5s.

Bright and Medd.—LIBER PRECUM PUBLICARUM ECCLESIÆ ANGLICANÆ. A GULIELMO BRIGHT, S.T.P., et PETRO GOLDSMITH MEDD, A.M., Latine redditus. [In hac Editione continentur Versiones Latinæ—1. Libri Precum Publicarum Ecclesiæ Anglicanæ ; 2. Liturgiæ Primæ Reformatæ ; 3. Liturgiæ Scoticanæ ; 4. Liturgiæ Americanæ.] *Small 8vo.* 7s. 6d.

Browne.—AN EXPOSITION OF THE THIRTY-NINE ARTICLES, Historical and Doctrinal. By E. H. BROWNE, D.D., formerly Bishop of Winchester. *8vo.* 16s.

Campion and Beamont.—THE PRAYER BOOK INTERLEAVED. With Historical Illustrations and Explanatory Notes arranged parallel to the Text. By W. M. CAMPION, D.D., and W. J. BEAMONT, M.A. *Small 8vo.* 7s. 6d.

Carter.—Works edited by the Rev. T. T. CARTER, M.A., Hon. Canon of Christ Church, Oxford.

THE TREASURY OF DEVOTION : a Manual of Prayer for General and Daily Use. Compiled by a Priest. *18mo.* 2s. 6d. ; *cloth limp,* 2s. ; *or bound with the Book of Common Prayer,* 3s. 6d. *Large-Type Edition. Crown 8vo.* 3s. 6d.

THE WAY OF LIFE : A Book of Prayers and Instruction for the Young at School, with a Preparation for Confirmation. Compiled by a Priest. *18mo.* 1s. 6d.

THE PATH OF HOLINESS : a First Book of Prayers, with the Service of the Holy Communion, for the Young. Compiled by a Priest. With Illustrations. *16mo.* 1s. 6d. ; *cloth limp,* 1s.

THE GUIDE TO HEAVEN : a Book of Prayers for every Want. (For the Working Classes.) Compiled by a Priest. *18mo.* 1s. 6d. ; *cloth limp,* 1s. *Large-Type Edition. Crown 8vo.* 1s. 6d. ; *cloth limp,* 1s.

[*continued.*

Carter.—Works edited by the Rev. T. T. CARTER, M.A., Hon. Canon of Christ Church, Oxford—*continued.*

SELF-RENUNCIATION. *16mo. 2s. 6d. Also the Larger Edition. Small 8vo. 3s. 6d.*

THE STAR OF CHILDHOOD; a First Book of Prayers and Instruction for Children. Compiled by a Priest. With Illustrations. *16mo. 2s. 6d.*

Carter.—MAXIMS AND GLEANINGS FROM THE WRITINGS OF T. T. CARTER, M.A. Selected and arranged for Daily Use. *Crown 16mo. 1s.*

Chandler.—THE SPIRIT OF MAN : An Essay in Christian Philosophy. By the Rev. A. CHANDLER, M.A., Rector of Poplar, E. *Crown 8vo. 5s.*

Conybeare and Howson.—THE LIFE AND EPISTLES OF ST. PAUL. By the Rev. W. J. CONYBEARE, M.A., and the Very Rev. J. S. HOWSON, D.D. With numerous Maps and Illustrations.

    LIBRARY EDITION. *Two Vols. 8vo. 21s.*
    STUDENT'S EDITION. *One Vol. Crown 8vo. 6s.*

Crake.—HISTORY OF THE CHURCH UNDER THE ROMAN EMPIRE, A.D. 30-476. By the Rev. A. D. CRAKE, B.A. *Crown 8vo. 7s. 6d.*

Devotional Series, 16mo, Red Borders. *Each 2s. 6d.*

BICKERSTETH'S YESTERDAY, TO-DAY, AND FOR EVER.
CHILCOT'S TREATISE ON EVIL THOUGHTS.
THE CHRISTIAN YEAR.
DEVOTIONAL BIRTHDAY BOOK.
HERBERT'S POEMS AND PROVERBS.
KEMPIS' (À) OF THE IMITATION OF CHRIST.
ST. FRANCIS DE SALES' THE DEVOUT LIFE.
WILSON'S THE LORD'S SUPPER. *Large type.*
*TAYLOR'S (JEREMY) HOLY LIVING.
* ———— ——— HOLY DYING.
    * *These two in one Volume. 5s.*

Devotional Series, 18mo, without Red Borders. *Each 1s.*

BICKERSTETH'S YESTERDAY, TO-DAY, AND FOR EVER.
THE CHRISTIAN YEAR.
HERBERT'S POEMS AND PROVERBS.
KEMPIS' (À) OF THE IMITATION OF CHRIST.
ST. FRANCIS DE SALES' THE DEVOUT LIFE.
WILSON'S THE LORD'S SUPPER. *Large type.*
*TAYLOR'S (JEREMY) HOLY LIVING.
* ———— ——— HOLY DYING.
    * *These two in one Volume. 2s. 6d.*

Edersheim.—Works by ALFRED EDERSHEIM, M.A., D.D., Ph.D., sometime Grinfield Lecturer on the Septuagint, Oxford.

THE LIFE AND TIMES OF JESUS THE MESSIAH. *Two Vols.* *8vo.* *24s.*

JESUS THE MESSIAH : being an Abridged Edition of 'The Life and Times of Jesus the Messiah.' *Crown 8vo.* *7s. 6d.*

PROPHECY AND HISTORY IN RELATION TO THE MESSIAH : The Warburton Lectures, 1880-1884. *8vo.* *12s.*

TOHU-VA-VOHU ('Without Form and Void') : being a collection of Fragmentary Thoughts and Criticism. *Crown 8vo.* *6s.*

Ellicott.—Works by C. J. ELLICOTT, D.D., Bishop of Gloucester and Bristol.

A CRITICAL AND GRAMMATICAL COMMENTARY ON ST. PAUL'S EPISTLES. Greek Text, with a Critical and Grammatical Commentary, and a Revised English Translation. *8vo.*

1 CORINTHIANS. *16s.*	PHILIPPIANS, COLOSSIANS, AND
GALATIANS. *8s. 6d.*	PHILEMON. *10s. 6d.*
EPHESIANS. *8s. 6d.*	THESSALONIANS. *7s. 6d.*
PASTORAL EPISTLES. *10s. 6d.*	

HISTORICAL LECTURES ON THE LIFE OF OUR LORD JESUS CHRIST. *8vo.* *12s.*

Epochs of Church History. Edited by MANDELL CREIGHTON, D.D., LL.D., Bishop of Peterborough. *Fcap.8vo.* *2s. 6d. each.*

THE ENGLISH CHURCH IN OTHER LANDS. By the Rev. H. W. TUCKER, M.A.

THE HISTORY OF THE RE-FORMATION IN ENGLAND. By the Rev. GEO. G. PERRY, M.A.

THE CHURCH OF THE EARLY FATHERS. By the Rev. ALFRED PLUMMER, D.D.

THE EVANGELICAL REVIVAL IN THE EIGHTEENTH CENTURY. By the Rev. J. H. OVERTON, M.A.

THE UNIVERSITY OF OXFORD. By the Hon. G. C. BRODRICK, D.C.L.

THE UNIVERSITY OF CAMBRIDGE. By J. BASS MULLINGER, M.A.

THE ENGLISH CHURCH IN THE MIDDLE AGES. By the Rev. W. HUNT, M.A.

THE CHURCH AND THE EASTERN EMPIRE. By the Rev. H. F. TOZER, M.A.

THE CHURCH AND THE ROMAN EMPIRE. By the Rev. A. CARR.

THE CHURCH AND THE PURITANS, 1570-1660. By HENRY OFFLEY WAKEMAN, M.A.

HILDEBRAND AND HIS TIMES. By the Rev. W. R. W. STEPHENS, M.A.

THE POPES AND THE HOHENSTAUFEN. By UGO BALZANI.

THE COUNTER-REFORMATION. By ADOLPHUS WILLIAM WARD, Litt. D.

WYCLIFFE AND MOVEMENTS FOR REFORM. By REGINALD L. POOLE, M.A.

THE ARIAN CONTROVERSY. By H. M. GWATKIN, M.A.

Fosbery.—Works edited by the Rev. THOMAS VINCENT FOSBERY, M.A., sometime Vicar of St. Giles's, Reading.

VOICES OF COMFORT. *Cheap Edition. Small 8vo.* 3s. 6d.
The Larger Edition (7s. 6d.) may still be had.

HYMNS AND POEMS FOR THE SICK AND SUFFERING. In connection with the Service for the Visitation of the Sick. Selected from Various Authors. *Small 8vo.* 3s. 6d.

Garland.—THE PRACTICAL TEACHING OF THE APO-CALYPSE. By the Rev. G. V. GARLAND, M.A. *8vo.* 16s.

Gore.—Works by the Rev. CHARLES GORE, M.A., Principal of the Pusey House ; Fellow of Trinity College, Oxford.

THE MINISTRY OF THE CHRISTIAN CHURCH. *8vo.* 10s. 6d.

ROMAN CATHOLIC CLAIMS. *Crown 8vo.* 3s. 6d.

Goulburn.—Works by EDWARD MEYRICK GOULBURN, D.D., D.C.L., sometime Dean of Norwich.

THOUGHTS ON PERSONAL RELIGION. *Small 8vo,* 6s. 6d. ; *Cheap Edition,* 3s. 6d. ; *Presentation Edition,* 2 vols. *small 8vo,* 10s. 6d.

THE PURSUIT OF HOLINESS : a Sequel to 'Thoughts on Personal Religion.' *Small 8vo.* 5s. *Cheap Edition,* 3s. 6d.

THE CHILD SAMUEL : a Practical and Devotional Commentary on the Birth and Childhood of the Prophet Samuel, as recorded in 1 Sam. i., ii. 1-27, iii. *Small 8vo.* 2s. 6d.

THE GOSPEL OF THE CHILDHOOD : a Practical and Devotional Commentary on the Single Incident of our Blessed Lord's Childhood (St. Luke ii. 41 to the end). *Crown 8vo.* 2s. 6d.

THE COLLECTS OF THE DAY : an Exposition, Critical and Devotional, of the Collects appointed at the Communion. With Preliminary Essays on their Structure, Sources, etc. *2 vols. Crown 8vo.* 8s. *each.*

THOUGHTS UPON THE LITURGICAL GOSPELS for the Sundays, one for each day in the year. With an Introduction on their Origin, History, the Modifications made in them by the Reformers and by the Revisers of the Prayer Book. *2 vols. Crown 8vo.* 16s.

MEDITATIONS UPON THE LITURGICAL GOSPELS for the Minor Festivals of Christ, the two first Week-days of the Easter and Whitsun Festivals, and the Red-letter Saints' Days. *Crown 8vo.* 8s. 6d.

FAMILY PRAYERS compiled from various sources (chiefly from Bishop Hamilton's Manual), and arranged on the Liturgical Principle. *Crown 8vo.* 3s. 6d. *Cheap Edition.* 16mo. 1s.

Harrison.—PROBLEMS OF CHRISTIANITY AND SCEPTI-CISM ; Lessons from Twenty Years' Experience in the Field of Christian Evidence. By the Rev. ALEXANDER J. HARRISON, B.D., Lecturer of the Christian Evidence Society. *Crown 8vo.* 7s. 6d.

Hernaman.—LYRA CONSOLATIONIS. From the Poets of the Seventeenth, Eighteenth, and Nineteenth Centuries. Selected and arranged by CLAUDIA FRANCES HERNAMAN. *Small 8vo.* 6s.

Holland.—Works by the Rev. HENRY SCOTT HOLLAND, M.A., Canon and Precentor of St. Paul's.

CREED AND CHARACTER : Sermons. *Crown 8vo.* 7s. 6d.

ON BEHALF OF BELIEF. Sermons preached in St. Paul's Cathedral. *Crown 8vo.* 6s.

CHRIST OR ECCLESIASTES. Sermons preached in St. Paul's Cathedral. *Crown 8vo.* 3s. 6d.

GOOD FRIDAY. Being Addresses on the Seven Last Words, delivered at St. Paul's Cathedral on Good Friday. *Small 8vo.* 2s.

LOGIC AND LIFE, with other Sermons. *Crown 8vo.* 7s. 6d.

Hopkins.—CHRIST THE CONSOLER. A Book of Comfort for the Sick. By ELLICE HOPKINS. *Small 8vo.* 2s. 6d.

Ingram.—HAPPINESS : In the Spiritual Life ; or, 'The Secret of the Lord.' A Series of Practical Considerations. By the Rev. W. CLAVELL INGRAM, M.A., Vicar of St. Matthew's, Leicester. *Crown 8vo.* 7s. 6d.

INHERITANCE, THE, OF THE SAINTS ; or, Thoughts on the Communion of Saints and the Life of the World to come. Collected chiefly from English Writers by L. P. With a Preface by the Rev. HENRY SCOTT HOLLAND, M.A. *Crown 8vo.* 7s. 6d.

Jameson.—Works by Mrs. JAMESON.

SACRED AND LEGENDARY ART, containing Legends of the Angels and Archangels, the Evangelists, the Apostles. With 19 etchings and 187 Woodcuts. *Two Vols. Cloth, gilt top,* 20s. *net.*

LEGENDS OF THE MONASTIC ORDERS, as represented in the Fine Arts. With 11 etchings and 88 Woodcuts. *One Vol. Cloth, gilt top,* 10s. *net.*

LEGENDS OF THE MADONNA, OR BLESSED VIRGIN MARY. With 27 Etchings and 165 Woodcuts. *One Vol. Cloth, gilt top,* 10s. *net.*

THE HISTORY OF OUR LORD, as exemplified in Works of Art. Commenced by the late Mrs. JAMESON ; continued and completed by LADY EASTLAKE. With 31 etchings and 281 Woodcuts. *Two Vols. 8vo.* 20s. *net.*

Jennings.—ECCLESIA ANGLICANA. A History of the Church of Christ in England from the Earliest to the Present Times. By the Rev. ARTHUR CHARLES JENNINGS, M.A. *Crown 8vo.* 7s. 6d.

Jukes.—Works by ANDREW JUKES.

THE NEW MAN AND THE ETERNAL LIFE. Notes on the Reiterated Amens of the Son of God. *Crown 8vo.* 6s.

THE NAMES OF GOD IN HOLY SCRIPTURE: a Revelation of His Nature and Relationships. *Crown 8vo.* 4s. 6d.

THE TYPES OF GENESIS. *Crown 8vo.* 7s. 6d.

THE SECOND DEATH AND THE RESTITUTION OF ALL THINGS. *Crown 8vo.* 3s. 6d.

THE MYSTERY OF THE KINGDOM. *Crown 8vo.* 2s. 6d.

Keble.—MAXIMS AND GLEANINGS FROM THE WRIT-INGS OF JOHN KEBLE, M.A. Selected and Arranged for Daily Use. By C. M. S. *Crown 16mo.* 1s.

SELECTIONS FROM THE WRITINGS OF JOHN KEBLE, M.A. *Crown 8vo.* 3s. 6d.

Kennaway.—CONSOLATIO ; OR, COMFORT FOR THE AFFLICTED. Edited by the late Rev. C. E. KENNAWAY. 16mo. 2s. 6d.

King.—DR. LIDDON'S TOUR IN EGYPT AND PALES-TINE IN 1886. Being Letters descriptive of the Tour, written by his Sister, Mrs. KING. *Crown 8vo.* 5s.

Knox Little.—Works by W. J. KNOX LITTLE, M.A., Canon Residentiary of Worcester, and Vicar of Hoar Cross.

THE CHRISTIAN HOME. *Crown 8vo.* 6s. 6d.

THE HOPES AND DECISIONS OF THE PASSION OF OUR MOST HOLY REDEEMER. *Crown 8vo.* 3s. 6d.

THE THREE HOURS' AGONY OF OUR BLESSED REDEEMER. Being Addresses in the form of Meditations delivered in St. Alban's Church, Manchester, on Good Friday. *Small 8vo.* 2s. ; *or in Paper Cover,* 1s.

CHARACTERISTICS AND MOTIVES OF THE CHRISTIAN LIFE. Ten Sermons preached in Manchester Cathedral, in Lent and Advent. *Crown 8vo.* 3s. 6d.

SERMONS PREACHED FOR THE MOST PART IN MANCHES-TER. *Crown 8vo.* 3s. 6d.

THE MYSTERY OF THE PASSION OF OUR MOST HOLY REDEEMER. *Crown 8vo.* 3s. 6d.

THE WITNESS OF THE PASSION OF OUR MOST HOLY REDEEMER. *Crown 8vo.* 3s. 6d.

THE LIGHT OF LIFE. Sermons preached on Various Occasions. *Crown 8vo.* 3s. 6d.

SUNLIGHT AND SHADOW IN THE CHRISTIAN LIFE. Sermons preached for the most part in America. *Crown 8vo.* 3s. 6d.

Lear.—Works by, and Edited by, H. L. SIDNEY LEAR.

FOR DAYS AND YEARS. A Book containing a Text, Short Reading, and Hymn for Every Day in the Church's Year. 16mo. 2s. 6d. *Also a Cheap Edition*, 32mo. 1s.; *or cloth gilt*, 1s. 6d.

FIVE MINUTES. Daily Readings of Poetry 16mo. 3s. 6d. *Also a Cheap Edition.* 32mo. 1s. ; *or cloth gilt*, 1s. 6d.

WEARINESS. A Book for the Languid and Lonely. *Large Type. Small 8vo.* 5s.

THE LIGHT OF THE CONSCIENCE. 16mo. 2s. 6d. 32mo. 1s. ; *cloth limp*, 6d.

CHRISTIAN BIOGRAPHIES. *Nine Vols. Crown 8vo.* 3s. 6d. *each.*

MADAME LOUISE DE FRANCE, Daughter of Louis XV., known also as the Mother Térèse de St. Augustin.

A DOMINICAN ARTIST: a Sketch of the Life of the Rev. Père Besson, of the Order of St. Dominic.

HENRI PERREYVE. By A. GRATRY.

ST. FRANCIS DE SALES, Bishop and Prince of Geneva.

THE REVIVAL OF PRIESTLY LIFE IN THE SEVENTEENTH CENTURY IN FRANCE.

A CHRISTIAN PAINTER OF THE NINETEENTH CENTURY.

BOSSUET AND HIS CONTEMPORARIES.

FÉNELON, ARCHBISHOP OF CAMBRAI.

HENRI DOMINIQUE LACORDAIRE.

DEVOTIONAL WORKS. Edited by H. L. SIDNEY LEAR. *New and Uniform Editions. Nine Vols.* 16mo. 2s. 6d. *each.*

FÉNELON'S SPIRITUAL LETTERS TO MEN.

FÉNELON'S SPIRITUAL LETTERS TO WOMEN.

A SELECTION FROM THE SPIRITUAL LETTERS OF ST. FRANCIS DE SALES.

THE SPIRIT OF ST. FRANCIS DE SALES.

THE HIDDEN LIFE OF THE SOUL.

THE LIGHT OF THE CONSCIENCE.

SELF-RENUNCIATION. From the French.

ST. FRANCIS DE SALES' OF THE LOVE OF GOD.

SELECTIONS FROM PASCAL'S THOUGHTS.

Library of Spiritual Works for English Catholics. *Original Edition. With Red Borders. Small 8vo.* 5s. *each. New and Cheaper Editions.* 16mo. 2s. 6d. *each.*

OF THE IMITATION OF CHRIST.

THE SPIRITUAL COMBAT. By LAURENCE SCUPOLI.

THE DEVOUT LIFE. By ST. FRANCIS DE SALES.

OF THE LOVE OF GOD. By ST. FRANCIS DE SALES.

THE CONFESSIONS OF ST. AUGUSTINE. *In Ten Books.*

THE CHRISTIAN YEAR. 5s. *Edition only*

Liddon.—Works by HENRY PARRY LIDDON, D.D., D.C.L., LL.D., late Canon Residentiary and Chancellor of St. Paul's.

SERMONS ON OLD TESTAMENT SUBJECTS. *Crown 8vo.* 5s.

SERMONS ON SOME WORDS OF CHRIST. *Crown 8vo.*

THE DIVINITY OF OUR LORD AND SAVIOUR JESUS CHRIST. Being the Bampton Lectures for 1866. *Crown 8vo.* 5s.

ADVENT IN ST. PAUL'S. Sermons bearing chiefly on the Two Comings of our Lord. *Two Vols. Crown 8vo.* 3s. 6d. *each. Cheap Edition in one Volume. Crown 8vo.* 5s.

CHRISTMASTIDE IN ST. PAUL'S. Sermons bearing chiefly on the Birth of our Lord and the End of the Year. *Crown 8vo.* 5s.

PASSIONTIDE SERMONS. *Crown 8vo.* 5s.

EASTER IN ST. PAUL'S. Sermons bearing chiefly on the Resurrection of our Lord. *Two Vols. Crown 8vo.* 3s. 6d. *each. Cheap Edition in one Volume. Crown 8vo.* 5s.

SERMONS PREACHED BEFORE THE UNIVERSITY OF OXFORD. *Two Vols. Crown 8vo.* 3s. 6d. *each. Cheap Edition in one Volume. Crown 8vo.* 5s.

THE MAGNIFICAT. Sermons in St. Paul's. *Crown 8vo.* 2s. 6d.

SOME ELEMENTS OF RELIGION. Lent Lectures. *Small 8vo.* 2s. 6d. ; *or in Paper Cover,* 1s. 6d.

The Crown 8vo Edition (5s.) *may still be had.*

SELECTIONS FROM THE WRITINGS OF H. P. LIDDON, D.D. *Crown 8vo.* 3s. 6d.

MAXIMS AND GLEANINGS FROM THE WRITINGS OF H. P. LIDDON, D.D. Selected and arranged by C. M. S. *Crown 16mo.* 1s.

DR. LIDDON'S TOUR IN EGYPT AND PALESTINE IN 1886. Being Letters descriptive of the Tour, written by his Sister, Mrs. KING. *Crown 8vo.* 5s.

Luckock.—Works by HERBERT MORTIMER LUCKOCK, D.D., Canon of Ely.

AFTER DEATH. An Examination of the Testimony of Primitive Times respecting the State of the Faithful Dead, and their Relationship to the Living. *Crown 8vo.* 6s.

THE INTERMEDIATE STATE BETWEEN DEATH AND JUDGMENT. Being a Sequel to *After Death. Crown 8vo.* 6s.

FOOTPRINTS OF THE SON OF MAN, as traced by St. Mark. Being Eighty Portions for Private Study, Family Reading, and Instructions in Church. *Two Vols. Crown 8vo.* 12s. *Cheap Edition in one Vol. Crown 8vo.* 5s.

[continued.

Luckock.—Works by HERBERT MORTIMER LUCKOCK, D.D., Canon of Ely—*continued.*

THE DIVINE LITURGY. Being the Order for Holy Communion, Historically, Doctrinally, and Devotionally set forth, in Fifty Portions. *Crown 8vo. 6s.*

STUDIES IN THE HISTORY OF THE BOOK OF COMMON PRAYER. The Anglican Reform—The Puritan Innovations—The Elizabethan Reaction—The Caroline Settlement. With Appendices. *Crown 8vo. 6s.*

THE BISHOPS IN THE TOWER. A Record of Stirring Events affecting the Church and Nonconformists from the Restoration to the Revolution. *Crown 8vo. 6s.*

LYRA APOSTOLICA. Poems by J. W. BOWDEN, R. H. FROUDE, J. KEBLE, J. H. NEWMAN, R. I. WILBERFORCE, and I. WILLIAMS; and a New Preface by CARDINAL NEWMAN. *16mo. With Red Borders. 2s. 6d.*

LYRA GERMANICA. Hymns translated from the German by CATHERINE WINKWORTH. *Small 8vo. 5s.*

MacColl.—CHRISTIANITY IN RELATION TO SCIENCE AND MORALS. By the Rev. MALCOLM MACCOLL, M.A., Canon Residentiary of Ripon. *Crown 8vo. 6s.*

Mason.—Works by A. J. MASON, D.D., formerly Fellow of Trinity College, Cambridge.

THE FAITH OF THE GOSPEL. A Manual of Christian Doctrine. *Crown 8vo. 7s. 6d. Also a Large-Paper Edition for Marginal Notes. 4to. 12s. 6d.*

THE RELATION OF CONFIRMATION TO BAPTISM. As taught in Holy Scripture and the Fathers. *Crown 8vo. 7s. 6d.*

Mercier.—OUR MOTHER CHURCH: Being Simple Talk on High Topics. By Mrs. JEROME MERCIER. *Small 8vo. 3s. 6d.*

Moberly.—Works by GEORGE MOBERLY, D.C.L., late Bishop of Salisbury.

PLAIN SERMONS. Preached at Brighstone. *Crown 8vo. 5s.*

THE SAYINGS OF THE GREAT FORTY DAYS, between the Resurrection and Ascension, regarded as the Outlines of the Kingdom of God. In Five Discourses. *Crown 8vo. 5s.*

PAROCHIAL SERMONS. Mostly preached at Brighstone. *Crown 8vo. 7s. 6d.*

SERMONS PREACHED AT WINCHESTER COLLEGE. *Two Vols. Small 8vo. 6s. 6d. each. Sold separately.*

Mozley.—Works by J. B. MOZLEY, D.D., late Canon of Christ Church, and Regius Professor of Divinity at Oxford.

ESSAYS, HISTORICAL AND THEOLOGICAL. *Two Vols. 8vo. 24s.*

EIGHT LECTURES ON MIRACLES. Being the Bampton Lectures for 1865. *Crown 8vo. 7s. 6d.*

RULING IDEAS IN EARLY AGES AND THEIR RELATION TO OLD TESTAMENT FAITH. Lectures delivered to Graduates of the University of Oxford. *8vo. 10s. 6d.*

SERMONS PREACHED BEFORE THE UNIVERSITY OF OXFORD, and on Various Occasions. *Crown 8vo. 7s. 6d.*

SERMONS, PAROCHIAL AND OCCASIONAL. *Crown 8vo. 7s. 6d.*

Mozley.—Works by the Rev. T. MOZLEY, M.A., Author of 'Reminiscences of Oriel College and the Oxford Movement.'

THE WORD. *Crown 8vo. 7s. 6d.*

THE SON. *Crown 8vo. 7s. 6d.*

LETTERS FROM ROME ON THE OCCASION OF THE ŒCUMENICAL COUNCIL 1869-1870. *Two Vols. Cr. 8vo. 18s.*

Newbolt.—Works by the Rev. W. C. E. NEWBOLT, M.A., Canon Residentiary of St. Paul's.

THE FRUIT OF THE SPIRIT. Being Ten Addresses bearing on the Spiritual Life. *Crown 8vo. 2s. 6d.*

THE MAN OF GOD. Being Six Addresses delivered during Lent 1886, at the Primary Ordination of the Right Rev. the Lord Alwyne Compton, D.D., Bishop of Ely. *Small 8vo. 1s. 6d.*

THE VOICE OF THE PRAYER BOOK. Being Spiritual Addresses bearing on the Book of Common Prayer. *Crown 8vo. 2s. 6d.*

Newnham.—THE ALL-FATHER: Sermons preached in a Village Church. By the Rev. H. P. NEWNHAM. With Preface by EDNA LYALL. *Crown 8vo. 4s. 6d.*

Newnham.—ALRESFORD ESSAYS FOR THE TIMES. By Rev. W. O. NEWNHAM, M.A., late Rector of Alresford. CONTENTS :— Bible Story of Creation—Bible Story of Eden—Bible Story of the Deluge—After Death—Miracles : A Conversation—Eternal Punishment —The Resurrection of the Body. *Crown 8vo. 6s.*

Newman.—Works by JOHN HENRY NEWMAN, B.D., sometime Vicar of St. Mary's, Oxford.

PAROCHIAL AND PLAIN SERMONS. *Eight Vols. Cabinet Edition. Crown 8vo. 5s. each. Popular Edition. Eight Vols. Crown 8vo. 3s. 6d. each.*

SELECTION, ADAPTED TO THE SEASONS OF THE ECCLE-SIASTICAL YEAR, from the 'Parochial and Plain Sermons.' *Cabinet Edition. Crown 8vo. 5s. Popular Edition. Crown 8vo. 3s. 6d.*

FIFTEEN SERMONS PREACHED BEFORE THE UNIVERSITY OF OXFORD, between A.D. 1826 and 1843. *Crown 8vo. 5s.*

SERMONS BEARING UPON SUBJECTS OF THE DAY. *Cabinet Edition. Crown 8vo. 5s. Popular Edition. Crown 8vo. 3s. 6d.*

LECTURES ON THE DOCTRINE OF JUSTIFICATION. *Crown 8vo. 5s.*

THE LETTERS AND CORRESPONDENCE OF JOHN HENRY NEWMAN DURING HIS LIFE IN THE ENGLISH CHURCH. With a Brief Autobiographical Memoir. Arranged and Edited by ANNE MOZLEY. *Two Vols. 8vo. 30s. net.*

** *For other Works by Cardinal Newman, see Messrs. Longmans & Co.'s Catalogue of Works in General Literature.*

Osborne.—Works by EDWARD OSBORNE, Mission Priest of the Society of St. John the Evangelist, Cowley, Oxford.

THE CHILDREN'S SAVIOUR. Instructions to Children on the Life of our Lord and Saviour Jesus Christ. *Illustrated. 16mo. 2s. 6d.*

THE SAVIOUR-KING. Instructions to Children on Old Testament Types and Illustrations of the Life of Christ. *Illustrated. 16mo. 2s. 6d.*

THE CHILDREN'S FAITH. Instructions to Children on the Apostles' Creed. *Illustrated. 16mo. 2s. 6d.*

Oxenden.—Works by the Right Rev. ASHTON OXENDEN, formerly Bishop of Montreal.

THE HISTORY OF MY LIFE : An Autobiography. *Crown 8vo. 5s.*

PEACE AND ITS HINDRANCES. *Crown 8vo. 1s. ; sewed, 2s., cloth.*

THE PATHWAY OF SAFETY ; or, Counsel to the Awakened. *Fcap. 8vo, large type. 2s. 6d. Cheap Edition. Small type, limp. 1s.*

THE EARNEST COMMUNICANT. *New Red Rubric Edition. 32mo, cloth. 2s. Common Edition. 32mo, 1s.*

OUR CHURCH AND HER SERVICES. *Fcap. 8vo. 2s. 6d.*

[*continued.*

Oxenden.—Works by the Right Rev. ASHTON OXENDEN, formerly Bishop of Montreal—*continued.*

FAMILY PRAYERS FOR FOUR WEEKS. First Series. *Fcap. 8vo.* 2s. 6d. Second Series. *Fcap. 8vo.* 2s. 6d.
LARGE TYPE EDITION. Two Series in one Volume. *Crown 8vo.* 6s.

COTTAGE SERMONS; or, Plain Words to the Poor. *Fcap. 8vo.* 2s. 6d.

THOUGHTS FOR HOLY WEEK. *16mo, cloth.* 1s. 6d.

DECISION. *18mo.* 1s. 6d.

THE HOME BEYOND; or, A Happy Old Age. *Fcap. 8vo.* 1s. 6d.

THE LABOURING MAN'S BOOK. *18mo, large type, cloth.* 1s. 6d.

Paget.—Works by FRANCIS PAGET, D.D., Dean of Christ Church, Oxford.

THE SPIRIT OF DISCIPLINE: Sermons. *Crown 8vo.* 6s. 6d.

FACULTIES AND DIFFICULTIES FOR BELIEF AND DIS-BELIEF. *Crown 8vo.* 6s. 6d.

THE HALLOWING OF WORK. Addresses given at Eton, January 16-18, 1888. *Small 8vo.* 2s.

PRACTICAL REFLECTIONS. By a CLERGYMAN. With Prefaces by H. P. LIDDON, D.D., D.C.L. *Crown 8vo.*

Vol. I.—THE HOLY GOSPELS. 4s. 6d.

Vol. II.—ACTS TO REVELATION. 6s.

THE PSALMS. 5s.

PRIEST (THE) TO THE ALTAR; Or, Aids to the Devout Celebration of Holy Communion, chiefly after the Ancient English Use of Sarum. *Royal 8vo.* 12s.

Pusey.—Works by E. B. PUSEY, D.D.

PRIVATE PRAYERS. With Preface by H. P. LIDDON, D.D. 32mo. 1s.

PRAYERS FOR A YOUNG SCHOOLBOY. With a Preface by H. P. LIDDON, D.D. 24mo. 1s.

SELECTIONS FROM THE WRITINGS OF EDWARD BOUVERIE PUSEY, D.D. *Crown 8vo.* 3s. 6d.

MAXIMS AND GLEANINGS FROM THE WRITINGS OF EDWARD BOUVERIE PUSEY, D.D. Selected and Arranged for Daily Use. By C. M. S. *Crown 16mo.* 1s.

Reynolds.—THE NATURAL HISTORY OF IMMORTALITY. By the Rev. J. W. REYNOLDS, M.A., Prebendary of St. Paul's. *Crown 8vo.* 7s. 6d.

Richmond.—C H R I S T I A N E C O N O M I C S. By the Rev.
WILFRID RICHMOND, M.A., sometime Warden of Trinity College.
Glenalmond. *Crown 8vo.* 6s.

Sanday.—THE ORACLES OF GOD : Nine Lectures on the
Nature and Extent of Biblical Inspiration and the Special Significance
of the Old Testament Scriptures at the Present Time. By W.
SANDAY, M.A., D.D., LL.D., Dean Ireland's Professor of Exegesis
and Fellow of Exeter College. *Crown 8vo.* 4s.

Seebohm.—THE OXFORD REFORMERS—JOHN COLET,
ERASMUS, AND THOMAS MORE : A History of their Fellow-
Work. By FREDERIC SEEBOHM. *8vo.* 14s.

Stanton.—THE PLACE OF AUTHORITY IN MATTERS
OF RELIGIOUS BELIEF. By VINCENT HENRY STANTON, D.D.,
Fellow of Trinity College, Ely Professor of Divinity, Cambridge.
Crown 8vo. 6s.

Stephen.—ESSAYS IN ECCLESIASTICAL BIOGRAPHY.
By the Right Hon. Sir J. STEPHEN. *Crown 8vo.* 7s. 6d.

Swayne.—THE BLESSED DEAD IN PARADISE. Four
All Saints' Day Sermons, preached in Salisbury Cathedral. By R. G.
SWAYNE, M.A. *Crown 8vo.* 3s. 6d.

Tweddell.—THE SOUL IN CONFLICT. A Practical Exami-
nation of some Difficulties and Duties of the Spiritual Life. By
MARSHALL TWEDDELL, M.A., Vicar of St. Saviour, Paddington.
Crown 8vo. 6s.

Twells.—COLLOQUIES ON PREACHING. By HENRY
TWELLS, M.A., Honorary Canon of Peterborough. *Crown 8vo.* 5s.

Wakeman.—THE HISTORY OF RELIGION IN ENGLAND.
By HENRY OFFLEY WAKEMAN, M.A. *Small 8vo.* 1s. 6d.

Welldon. — THE FUTURE AND THE PAST. Sermons
preached to Harrow Boys. By the Rev. J. E. C. WELLDON, M.A.,
Head Master of Harrow School. *Crown 8vo.* 7s. 6d.

Williams.—Works by the Rev. ISAAC WILLIAMS, B.D.
A DEVOTIONAL COMMENTARY ON THE GOSPEL NARRA-
TIVE. *Eight Vols. Crown 8vo.* 5s. *each. Sold separately.*

THOUGHTS ON THE STUDY OF THE HOLY GOSPELS.	OUR LORD'S MINISTRY (Third Year).
A HARMONY OF THE FOUR GOSPELS.	THE HOLY WEEK.
OUR LORD'S NATIVITY.	OUR LORD'S PASSION.
OUR LORD'S MINISTRY(Second Year).	OUR LORD'S RESURRECTION.

FEMALE CHARACTERS OF HOLY SCRIPTURE. A Series of
Sermons. *Crown 8vo.* 5s.

[*continued.*

Williams.—Works by the Rev. ISAAC WILLIAMS, B.D., formerly Fellow of Trinity College, Oxford—*continued.*

THE CHARACTERS OF THE OLD TESTAMENT. A Series of Sermons. *Crown 8vo. 5s.*

THE APOCALYPSE. With Notes and Reflections. *Crown 8vo. 5s.*

SERMONS ON THE EPISTLES AND GOSPELS FOR THE SUNDAYS AND HOLY DAYS THROUGHOUT THE YEAR. *Two Vols. Crown 8vo. 5s. each.*

PLAIN SERMONS ON THE CATECHISM. *Two Vols. Crown 8vo. 5s. each.*

SELECTIONS FROM THE WRITINGS OF ISAAC WILLIAMS, B.D. *Crown 8vo. 3s. 6d.*

Woodford.—Works by JAMES RUSSELL WOODFORD, D.D., sometime Lord Bishop of Ely.

THE GREAT COMMISSION. Twelve Addresses on the Ordinal. Edited, with an Introduction on the Ordinations of his Episcopate, by HERBERT MORTIMER LUCKOCK, D.D. *Crown 8vo. 5s.*

SERMONS ON OLD AND NEW TESTAMENT SUBJECTS. Edited by HERBERT MORTIMER LUCKOCK, D.D. *Crown 8vo. 5s.*

Woodruff.—THE CHILDREN'S YEAR. Verses for the Sundays and Holy Days throughout the Year. By C. H. WOODRUFF, B.C.L. With an Introduction by the LORD BISHOP OF SOUTHWELL. *Fcap. 8vo. 3s. 6d.*

Wordsworth.

For List of Works by the late Christopher Wordsworth, D.D., Bishop of Lincoln, see Messrs. Longmans & Co.'s Catalogue of Theological Works, 32 pp. Sent post free on application.

Wordsworth.—Works by ELIZABETH WORDSWORTH, Principal of Lady Margaret Hall, Oxford.

ILLUSTRATIONS OF THE CREED. *Crown 8vo. 5s.*

CHRISTOPHER AND OTHER POEMS. *Crown 8vo. 6s.*

Younghusband.—Works by FRANCES YOUNGHUSBAND.

THE STORY OF OUR LORD, told in Simple Language for Children. With 25 Illustrations from Pictures by the Old Masters. *Crown 8vo. 2s. 6d.*

THE STORY OF GENESIS, told in Simple Language for Children. *Crown 8vo. 2s. 6d.*

THE STORY OF THE EXODUS, told in Simple Language for Children. With Map and 29 Illustrations. *Crown 8vo. 2s. 6d.*

Printed by T. and A. CONSTABLE, Printers to Her Majesty, *at the Edinburgh University Press.*

20,000/12/91.